FORWARD

I knew nothing about horses, and didn't ever expect to know anything about horses, until I married my wife (and editor), Gretchen. Forty-three years and forty-seven horses later, I can only say that it's been one heck of a ride, and I still have a lot to learn about my four-footed obsession! We started out with one backyard hunter-jumper and now, at last count, administer to fifteen racehorses and one retired gelding that once jumped over the moon. There are not enough words and phrases in Roget's Thesaurus to describe the total experience, which includes relating to horses and relating to people who relate to horses. But I thought I'd give it a try and made up a few stories for your amusement and maybe even a little insight into the horse world.

You may think you know some of the characters in these tales, or even think that you *are* one of the characters. So I must assure you that neither you, your horse, nor anyone else living on the face of this planet is depicted herein, and any semblance to anybody, living or dead, is purely coincidental. Bull Head is one of two exceptions to my disclaimer. This tale is loosely based on a factual historical event, but I seriously doubt that the horse's vocabulary was as broad as I have implied. The other exception is the use of familiar Revolutionary War names in the *Highwayman*. Their part in the story is entirely fictional.

I have written other fictional short stories, many with horses as the theme. These can be found in *Ten Tall Tales by R*

D Weilburg, a book published earlier with a variety of themes. I have reprinted one of these tales, *The Leetle Horse*, as a bonus to tweak your interest in that publication. This explains why there are actually eleven stories in *Ten Horse Tales by R D Weilburg*. I sincerely hope you enjoy each and every one!

    R D Weilburg 2009

Other books by R D Weilburg:

Prophecy's Heir
The Kyrid Legacy, Sequel to Prophecy's Heir
Ten Tall Tales

All books by R D Weilburg are available at Amazon.com

Prophecy's Challenge, a sequel to *Prophecy's Heir* and *The Kyrid Legacy* is in progress

TABLE OF CONTENTS

The Claimer 1

When Bijou Ate The Beanbot Jewels 13

The Catchcolt 31

Reggie's Regiment 43

Wind 73

The One That Got Away 89

The Highwayman 101

Got Your Goat 137

Reflections Of A Warhorse 155

One Day Of Not Playing Fair With Zachary 171

The Leetle Horse (reprinted) 195

THE CLAIMER

Skeeter Perez accepted his check from the Horseman's Bookkeeper and scrutinized it carefully. Two hundred and forty dollars could be the last sum he would ever withdraw from his racing account; the remaining sixty dollars would be going for the jockey's fee for his next, and probably last, race.

"You doin' okay, Skeeter?" the bookkeeper asked kindly.

"Oh, yeah, I'm fine Bess, thank you. I was just making sure that I still had enough money in the account for my jock mount."

"You gonna race old Beer Belly this weekend?"

"Fraid so, Bess. I'm sending him in a cheap claimer. I can't afford to keep him any more, so maybe somebody with a little money can take him on."

The bookkeeper reached over the counter and patted the diminutive horseman's arm. "Well, good luck to you, Skeeter. Give Marisa a hug for me."

"Thank you, Bess; I will." The weathered-faced trainer smiled as he turned to walk over to the Racing Secretary's office to enter his horse.

The smile that Bess returned was one of genuine friendship and respect for a man who had spent his life on the fringes of the Sport of Kings, and whose luck had finally worn thin to the point of giving up.

Alberto Perez had arrived on the racing scene as a wiry little seventeen-year-old jockey who could eat anything he wanted and never weigh in over a hundred pounds. Naturally, he was saddled with a mosquito-proportioned nickname, Skeeter, to match his skinny physique. Unfortunately Skeeter's bones broke about as often as he hit the turf with his body, and his girlfriend, Maria, said she wouldn't marry him unless he chose another facet of the horse game. He switched to assistant training, married Maria, and dreamt of the day when he'd have his own training stable.

Maria and Skeeter were frugal with their money, and by age thirty they had bought a little house on ten acres of flat land and had begun to build their dream equestrian facility. Their daughter, Marisa, was born about that time, and life became idyllic as Skeeter's family, horse farm, and training business flourished. Skeeter's horses won races, and his owner-clients paid handsomely for his expertise, so he invested in his own bloodstock and began to win races for himself.

Marisa was nine years old when Beer Belly was born, and she loved the little plain bay colt. She would go out to his paddock every day after school and groom him until his dappled rump glistened in the Texas sun. By the time he was a yearling he was as tame as a puppy, but he grew large and strong from exercise and nutrition provided by his attentive breeder's daughter. Skeeter and Maria marveled at how docile the colt was, and Beer Belly was given a reprieve from the usually requisite gelding procedure. The colt trained well, and, as a two-year-old, won his first race by six lengths.

But the joy of that homebred victory was bittersweet, because, on that same day, Maria was diagnosed with cancer. It would be a malignancy that could not be cured by surgery, medicine, prayer or love.

As medical bills mounted, Skeeter sold off all the horses he owned except Beer Belly, who continued to win races often enough to pay some of the medical and stable expenses. Over a period of three years Maria's health deteriorated to its finality, and Skeeter Perez gave up one owner after another because he didn't have the time to give enough attention to their racing stock to produce the winners that the horse game was all about. When Maria died, Skeeter was left with no clients, his little farm, fourteen-year-old Marisa, and a five-year-old racehorse that seemed beyond his prime. He took a hard look at his situation and decided that it was time to seek employment outside of the equine industry.

Skeeter Perez knew that any number of owners might pay five thousand dollars to claim Beer Belly, but they wouldn't pay any more than six thousand to buy him outright. Perez reasoned that if he ran him in a five thousand dollar claiming race and won it, he would get three thousand dollars for the win in addition to the five thousand he would get if his horse were claimed. A total of eight thousand dollars would give him a nice nest egg to live on until he found a job beyond the fence that surrounded the racetrack; he would even have enough money to start a college fund for Marisa, for whom he wanted a more prosperous life than she might encounter around the race barns. Of course, someone would have to claim Beer Belly, and Beer Belly would have to win.

Beer Belly was a sprint horse, and for some innate reason he sensed that he needed to run this six furlongs very fast. The Saturday night crowd cheered, Skeeter and Marisa screamed until their lungs ached, and the big bay won his race by a nose. Again the win was bittersweet; as they stood in the winner's circle for the celebratory photograph, Skeeter Perez eyed the claiming tag that the steward's assistant had attached to Beer Belly's halter, and he couldn't hold back his tears. He hugged his joyful daughter as

Beer Belly was led, prancing proudly because the fuss over him, to the testing barn by his new trainer.

"Bob Norton is a wonderful horseman," Skeeter said to Marisa. "He will take good care of Beer Belly, and he will send him to a good home when his career is over. Now come along, Honey, and lets clean out our tack room."

***

On Sunday morning, Skeeter decided to take Marisa to the track commissary for breakfast, and then go to the church service that the track Chaplain conducted for the backside employees. They had done this every Sunday when Maria was alive, and though he was leaving the racing business, Skeeter thought that continuing his Sunday services at the track would be a good way to stay in touch with his old friends in the horse community. Besides that, he had spent almost every Sunday morning of his adulthood at the track chapel, and he had no desire to go looking for a new church at this difficult juncture in his life.

The trainer and his daughter were patently morose as they picked over their breakfast. Skeeter explained to fourteen year-old Marisa that he was putting half of the eight thousand dollars they had earned the night before into a college account for her, and that money was sacrosanct. It was not going to be squandered on clothes or cars or horses or anything else not pertaining to the educational process. Moreover, he was going to sell his little farm and buy a small house somewhere near his next job and also close to the community college, so they could both focus on their future objectives. Marisa didn't cry, and Skeeter was relieved about that, because he didn't want to cry, either.

Then Bob Norton and Dr. Whibble, a veterinarian who was famous for his surgical prowess, came into the commissary and began searching faces. Cal Carranza, Bob Norton's trainer, followed them in. Their eyes caught Skeeter Perez just as his eyes caught sight of them, and all three quickly walked over to his booth and asked if they could talk for a moment.

Skeeter beckoned for them to sit, and his heart began to pound as he wondered what had gone wrong that would bring three eminent horsemen to his table less than twelve hours after one of them had claimed his horse.

Dr. Whibble smiled pleasantly, Carranza was expressionless, and Bob Norton looked dejected.

"What's up, fellas?" Skeeter asked anxiously. "Is something wrong with my horse?"

"Actually," Bob Norton said with a grimace, "something is wrong with *my* horse. He apparently chipped his knee pretty badly as he finished the race last night."

"Oh, jeez, I'm sorry to hear that, Mr. Norton," Skeeter said with surprise and concern. "Old Beer Belly's always been sound as a dollar."

"I know that, Skeeter, or I wouldn't have claimed him," Bob Norton answered sanguinely. "I don't claim horses from trainers who aren't considerate of their animals. It was the luck of the draw, and I drew the short straw. It's happened before, and it'll happen again."

Skeeter looked over to Dr. Whibble. "Can he be fixed?"

"Quite easily," the veterinarian answered pleasantly, "but it will take a minimum of four months after surgery before he can train again, and probably ten more weeks after that to get back in condition."

Bob Norton finally smiled, too. "My racing program doesn't include repair and rehabilitation, Skeeter. I don't own a physical stable. All of my horses are at the track or at the training center. I can't put this horse in my living room, so I want to give him back to you.

Skeeter did a double take, and looked at the new owner quizzically.

"I said *give*, Skeeter. He doesn't fit in my program, so I'll take the five K loss if you'll take him back. I want to cut any further expenditures right here. You can fix him or retire him to your place or whatever you want to do with him. He's yours if you'll take him."

"How much will it cost to fix him?" Marisa blurted.

"About two thousand dollars, plus a few bandages and poultices and lots of personal care," Dr. Whibble answered.

"I...I don't see how I could afford to take him back," Skeeter groused. I don't have a racing barn anymore, so I don't have any income. I have a child to feed and educate."

Tears suddenly welled in Marisa's eyes. "We couldn't fix Mommy, but we *could* fix Beer Belly, Daddy. I don't care about going to college. I want this part of my family back. Please, Daddy; I promise to take care of him and go to school, too."

"I need an assistant trainer," Cal Carranza said. "You can start tomorrow, and when you get back on your feet financially, I won't begrudge you if you start training for yourself. You don't need to be leaving us, Skeeter. You've been on the track too long to try something else. Take Beer Belly home and come to work here tomorrow."

Skeeter grinned. "I'll wait till Dr. Whibble fixes him before I take him home. Then you've got to attend him before and after school, Marisa. It looks like Beer Belly's going to be your new career."

Everyone seated at the booth sighed with relief as Marisa hugged her wiry little daddy. Bob Norton signed Beer Belly's

Jockey Club certificate back over to Alberto Perez, and they all got up and walked over to the backside church service together.

***

Marisa did as she had promised. She changed bandages and groomed Beer Belly before sunup every morning, and then went to school. She came home to feed Beer Belly, hand walk him according to the vet's instructions, and then spend the rest of the evening doing homework. After forty-five days, she began to turn the horse out every afternoon, and she stood and watched his every move to assure he wouldn't injure himself.

The Houston Thoroughbred race meet started in November, and Skeeter Perez had to move there to earn his living as assistant trainer to Cal Carranza. Marisa, who was turning fifteen, had to change schools, but she was willing to do that because Skeeter let her bring Beer Belly to the Houston track. The rehabilitated horse was ready to resume training.

Marisa came to the track at five o'clock every morning to help her father manage the stable. Skeeter drove her to school later in the morning, and picked her up after school to do more chores in the stalls. This system worked satisfactorily to keep the pretty and bright teenager focused on horses and school and avoid other bothersome distractions of the sort that make single fathers worry about their daughters. Skeeter always scheduled Beer Belly's workouts early enough in the day that Marisa could watch them and delight in his progress before she left for school.

By the first week in February, Beer Belly was ready to run in his first post-surgical race. It was a starter allowance restricted to horses that had run for five thousand dollars or less in claiming races during the last calendar year. Beer Belly proved that rehabilitative efforts had been worth the time and expense;

he won the five-furlong race handily and earned a six thousand dollar purse for his ecstatic owners.

Cal Carranza grinned as he joined his assistant in the winner's circle. "You'd better not run this horse in another claimer, Skeeter, or Bob Norton will buy him again."

"No way," Skeeter laughed. "It's allowance races from now on!"

"You ought to nominate him for the Claiming Crown in July," Carranza said. "Minnesota's not too far to van him from Dallas."

"Oh, yes, Daddy, let's do that!" Marisa chimed in. "School will be out, and the Dallas meet will be just ending. We could go there before we moved back home to San Antonio."

"Not a bad idea," Skeeter answered, but he frowned when he realized that the Houston meet was almost over. Very shortly he would be moving his little family two hundred and fifty miles north to the Dallas-Fort Worth Metroplex. That meant that his daughter would be changing schools again, and he would be away from his little farm near San Antonio for another four months. He had no owner-clients, and his winnings from this one race were not enough to tide him over while he reestablished his own training stable, so he couldn't leave his assistant job just yet. "Maybe he'll earn enough money in Dallas to pay for the gas," he added.

***

By the end of June, the Perez family's fortune had taken a solid turn for the better. In spite of moving to a new school near the end of the semester, Marisa completed her tenth grade studies near the top of her class. And, because of Skeeter's good management, the Dallas contingency of Carranza's racing organization had a very successful meet; Skeeter's own horse had contributed to the bevy of wins. Skeeter collected his last paycheck from Cal Carranza in the third week of July, paid a professional hauler to take Beer Belly to Minnesota, and followed the van north to the Claiming Crown races.

Since Beer Belly had been raced and claimed for five thousand dollars the year before, he was eligible for several of the races in the Claiming Crown series. This popular series of races was known nationally at the "Blue Collar" horseracing event, because only claimers that had run for a tag of thirty-five thousand dollars or less could participate. These were the workhorses that made up the vast majority of racing Thoroughbreds in the United States, and there was rarely an entrant who had been famous in his prime. The best part about these high dollar restricted stakes races was that the claimers running couldn't be claimed. Skeeter had decided that the six-furlong sprint race on the dirt was the best one for his horse, and the winner's portion of the seventy-five thousand dollar purse would be a hefty forty-five thousand.

The grandstand was full of average folks who had come to see the best of the average horses strut their stuff, and Marisa wandered through the crowds hoping that Beer Belly would become the focus of their attention after the starting gate opened. She was too short to see over the fans into the saddling paddock, but after the jockeys were legged up onto their mounts she recognized her father's green and yellow silks and followed their horse and rider to the track for the post parade. Skeeter found Marisa as the pony horse led Beer Belly onto the track, and they quickly walked to the grandstand where they could get a good view of the race.

Because the race was short, the starting gate was on the backstretch, and there would be only one sweeping turn before the horses came down the final stretch to the finish line. Skeeter

Perez had instructed his jockey to break out in front, set the pace around the turn, and then try to stay just in front of any closers. The horse and rider team knew what had to be done, and they did it. Two closers tried to pass Beer Belly on the stretch, but his last-ditch turn of foot was more than they could overcome as he led them over the wire. Beer Belly won by a neck, the crowd went wild, and Skeeter and Marisa wiped back tears of joy as they headed to the winner's circle. Their old rehabilitated claimer had won the race of his life, and of Skeeter's, and of Marisa's. The farm near San Antonio was going to become the headquarters of a racing stable again because of Beer Belly's exceptional effort in his last two strides of racing.

***

As Skeeter wrapped his horse's legs for the trip back to Texas, he noticed a little swelling in the right foreleg. He patted Beer Belly on his dappled rump and mumbled "thank you" to him as he ambled up the ramp into the van. The experienced trainer suspected that Beer Belly would arrive home in a less than sound state, and he was correct. In San Antonio, the big bay limped off the van, and though he ran happily in his old familiar paddock, he did not move soundly.

The next day, Skeeter drove to the track in San Antonio, but he didn't take Beer Belly or Marisa with him. He returned quite late in the afternoon, and Marisa was worried about what kept him at the track so long when he didn't have any horses there yet. He sat down at the dinner table in a strangely solemn mood.

Skeeter frowned as he picked over his dinner. "Beer Belly has probably chipped his other knee," he said. "I'm not going to have him fixed, and he's never going to race again."

Marisa daubed at her eyes with her napkin. "He's part of our family, Daddy. What will happen to him?"

"Well, he won't have to do anything he doesn't want to do any more. We'll turn him out to pasture, and Mother Nature will mend his injury quickly. He won't be hurting, because he won't be training. He'll be happy as a yearling colt out there in his old pasture. We're going to have to build a special stall and paddock for him, though, because he's a stallion. We've got to get that done in the next four months, because the new horses will be coming in December and January."

Marisa's eyes widened. "What new horses, Daddy? What did you do today?"

"Well, Honey, I had a long visit with Bob Norton." Skeeter began to smile coyly. "He's going to bring some retiring mares from Florida over here so Beer Belly can sire him a few claimers. He loves to run claimers; says he can make more money than running fussy fragile stakes horses. And I thought you might like to raise a new foal of your own, so I bought a stakes-winning mare to breed to Beer Belly just for us. You'll be eighteen by the time that foal is ready to race, so we'll register him with you being the breeder and owner."

Marisa happily understood that the Perez family enterprise was about to enter a rewarding and pleasurable new era.

***

Veterinary Doctor Marisa Perez is now in partnership with her successful father in an expanded Thoroughbred breeding and training facility. Beer Belly is still considered to be an integral part of the Perez family. He has never produced a graded stakes runner, but his Blue Collar babies are usually first to the wire in the races that the fans love to watch. Skeeter, Marisa, Bob Norton and, assuredly, Beer Belly are very happy about that.

WHEN BIJOU ATE THE BEANBOT JEWELS

There are hundreds of first-rate show-horse barns scattered across the United States in or near every city. The loyal boarders and trainees at every barn will insist, with shrewd but subtle encouragement by their handsome Director-of-All-Things-Equestrian, that their barn is unique, and death beneath the pounding feet of an angry hippopotamus would be preferable to relocating to any other show barn within a thousand miles of the current premises. This is because each fawning boarder dreams of the day when his or her horse is the leading Gleaner-of-Championships at the barn, which equates to being the favorite customer of said god-like trainer. For most boarding customers these dreams are fraught with frustration, because the reigning Gleaner-of-Championships and perpetual favorite of the worshipful trainer always seems to be a drop-dead-gorgeous blonde who is incredibly rich, agile as a cat, charming beyond all described criteria for gracefulness and poise, and jealous of her status in the barn's hierarchy to the point of casual homicide. Quant "Always" Cope was the Olympics medal winner and revered trainer at Fairy Ring Stables, and his *socialités du jour* were the Countess Ilsa Poletska and her magnificent gray jumper,

Bijou. They fit this pattern perfectly, and a good tale had to come of it.

Cope had indeed earned his way to equestrian loftiness by applying his natural riding ability to the talents of fine jumping stock that his future father-in-law magnanimously provided. He had started out as a successful rodeo rider and became the darling of the Grand Prix set when he met and ultimately married Sarah, whose dowry included a fifty-stall stable with an enormous indoor arena. He had assumed the nickname "Always" early in his career, because the name Quant Cope sounded too much like "can't cope," and he quickly tired of the snide ribbings from the cowboys on the rodeo circuit. Sarah, a perpetually sunburned horse-crazy tomboy type who smoked two packs of cigarettes a day, had very little riding talent, but she managed Fairy Ring Stables adroitly and cleverly manipulated the social pirouetting amongst the boarding customers. The boarders, women and men alike, all coveted the attention of Always Cope.

Ilsa Poletska was the customer who launched Always Cope's training-for-profit career. She brought eight fine Thoroughbreds and European Warmbloods, with their substantial boarding and training revenue stream, to Fairy Ring Stables on the day it opened for business. Sarah's daddy was impressed that his daughter and son-in-law were actually making money instead of spending it, so he deeded the arena to them as a wedding present. Ilsa Poletska was thus the instant favorite customer of the famous and ambitious trainer and his rather ordinary wife.

Countess Poletska, an ostensibly rich widow who owned a magnificent restaurant, was perfect for her role. She was a contrived blonde, about thirty-five, regal in features, and spoke with an Eastern European accent similar to Zsa Zsa Gabor's. Her riding apparel was outré, and she sported it with elegance; no sweat ever adorned her perfectly tanned forehead, and no dust or dung dared to tarnish her imported French calf boots. Her countenance graced the social pages of the newspaper every Sunday and regularly smiled from lesser tabloids during the week. The letters "BLUE" on the personalized license plates of her Rolls Royce reminded all sycophants of the richness of her blood and the celestial height of her social status. Her blue-blooded horses were as perfectly conformed as equines could be, because Always Cope had helped her to select them to amaze the social set, who generally know little about horses but hold the expensive creatures in awe and esteem. Countess Poletska was the darling of the barn and of the community's society, and only a few of Trainer Cope's employees knew that she was barely aware of which end of a horse was meant to be fed. It wasn't until her unbeaten Grand Prix jumper, Bijou, inadvertently insinuated himself into the socio-economic facet of her life that the true persona of the Countess was bared for all to see.

The annual charity ball at the exclusive Grand Chose Country Club was the event that allowed the city's social mavens to exhibit their resplendence to the fawning media, and Ilsa Poletska drew the top spot as hostess of the affair. The theme for the gala would be "Equestrian Elegance," and the Countess delighted the Planning Committee when she announced that she would be bringing her champion jumper, Bijou, to the ball. To make the event even more spectacular, she would ride the horse into the ballroom, and she would be showcasing her diamond earrings that had once belonged to the Queen of Poland, who was a not-so-distant relative. The social media were ecstatic, of course, and announced to all society-conscious subscribers that "Equestrian Elegance" was going to be the glitziest charity event that the entire state had ever witnessed because Countess Ilsa Poletska was starring.

Always Cope was somewhat perturbed when he read about Bijou the Horse's scheduled appearance at a human social event, because Ilsa Poletska had not bothered to discuss the matter with him before making a commitment that would involve his expertise. Always Cope also had to keep in mind that his whimsical client was his main meal ticket.

"By what sophistry, Sweet Madam Ilsa, do you expect to ride your white steed into a gaggle of screaming socialites and not leave them wading in an appetite-suppressing pile of horse doodoo?"

"Vhat? You mean he'd do *zat* in a formal ballroom?"

"He does it in his stall ten times a day, Ilsa! He even does it in his feed bucket when he's agitated. What makes you think he'd spare the hoity-toity of Grand Chose elite? I'm going to have to employ a cast of thousands to keep him proper while he's exposed to the City's Finest!" Always Cope loved hyperbole, and he had the Countess's attention.

"Oh, Alvays! I yust know yoo can solve zis lil problem for me! Ve can make a nice lil voooden road for him to valk on, and ve can make a lil paddock yust for him, mit a table and canapés and stuff like zat, no?"

"You'll have to invite some of my assistants, Ilsa. This will take a coordinated effort, or you could end up really embarrassed."

"Oh, please, Alvays! Surely yoo can do zis for me mitout a bunch of Hispanics, can't yoo? Zay don't haf za proper *couture*, yoo know."

"You want me to leave my best horsemen at home while your big clod tries to kick over and poop on the social elite of the community?"

"Vell, zay can come over early and erect ze voooden road and ze lil paddock before ze real peoples get to ze party, and zen leaf quickly, don't yoo sink, Alvays?"

Always grinned when he shook his head head. "Last week Sarah and I paid a thousand dollars for our ticket to that ball. I am not going to stand there all night and hold a horse for you, Ilsa. You're going to have to invite Trey and Jennifer to handle him for you. You can't just leave your big dumb horse wandering around a roomful of social wheels at the Grand Chose Country Club."

Trey was the assistant trainer at Fairy Ring Stables, and Jennifer was one of those horse-crazy girls that would rather work at a stable for minimum wage than go to college. Both were extremely knowledgeable about horse care, and they both spoke a smattering of Spanish, which made them invaluable to Always Cope as intermediaries between himself and the Hispanic laborers that were the backbone of the stable's staff. They happened to walk into the tack room as Cope and the Countess were conversing.

The Countess had always been civil to the young assistants, but she never had the slightest desire to socialize with them. She was shorter in stature than either of them, but she looked down her nose at them as she sized them up. "Zat could voork," she stated with an assuring nod. "Trey and Yennifer, voould yoo like to come to the Grand Chose Ball as guests of Bijou?"

Both of the young people smiled with surprise.

"Thank you, Countess Poletska, I certainly would!" Trey exclaimed.

"I'd love to come," Jennifer gushed almost simultaneously. "Thank you so much!"

"Um, yoo doo have some proper attire for zis kind of affair, doo yoo not? It's a wery proper soiree, yoo understand."

"I happen to have a tux squirreled away in my closet," Trey said with a chuckle. "Only been in it once, but I'm sure it still fits."

"I'll come up with something appropriate," the sandy-haired young woman said, still grinning. "I've dreamed about going to the Grand Chose Charity Ball since I was a little girl. It's on my birthday this year, if you can believe it! I'm ecstatic!"

The Countess allowed herself a condescending smile. "And yoo von't mind leading Bijou into ze ballroom mit me in a sidesaddle, vill yoo?"

"I think that would be a lot of fun!" Jennifer said genuinely. "Bijou is so regal, and so are you,"

"Ah, yes. Yoo are soo right. It vill be a charming evening! And, Alvays, I doo hope yoo'll work out all ze details mit zeese people. I doo haf so many ozzer sings to doo, yoo know." Then, without uttering another mispronounced syllable, she walked out to her Rolls with the elegance of a runway model.

Both Always and Trey followed every sensuous step she took with transfixed yearning until she had planted her elegant derriere into the driver's seat and closed the car door. Their expressions were sheepish when they turned to face a smirking, and unquestionably envious, Jennifer.

***

Always Cope told Trey and Jennifer how he wanted to set up the Countess's grand entrance, and they went about creating a walkway from a side entrance of the ballroom to one side of the dance floor. They paved the walkway and a small paddock at the end of it with plywood and covered the surfaces with six inches of pine shavings for a special stable effect. They lined Bijou's walkway and paddock with white cavaletti poles, which were set to twelve inches in height. This fence would establish boundaries for Bijou, but would allow partygoers to step over to pet him and get photo ops to commemorate their encounter with the gala's theme mascot. One of the grooms suggested that they place Mexican luminarias along the walkway for a dazzling lighting effect for the Countess's fairyland entrance.

Jennifer spent two weeks' salary for her tastefully flowered ankle-length dress, which was fortunately on sale at Penny's. It was her dream of a lifetime to lead a beautiful horse with an elegant rider into a regal affair. She was so happy to be there that being a chic mouse was amply satisfying for the opportunity to be in the same cosmic frame as the Cinderella Countess and Bijou, her magnificent jumping horse.

On the night of the charity gala, the paying guests had arrived and were partying with joyous abandon when the van from Fairy Ring Stables arrived at the side entrance to the ballroom of the Grand Chose Country Club. Trey and Jennifer, fully dressed for the formal affair, helped a groom to get Bijou out of the van and into the entryway. Jennifer had spent three hours braiding Bijou's dark mane and shampooing his long white tail, and he was resplendent as he pranced out of the van. They then met Countess Poletska as she stepped from her chauffeured Rolls Royce and assisted her onto the elegantly appointed dapple-gray horse. The smiling assistant trainers led the well-behaved jumper champion and his side-saddled passenger through the entrance and into the ballroom, where all the celebrants had gathered along the artificial saddle path to cheer their incredibly charming hostess.

Always and Sarah Cope stepped into the little flower-bedecked paddock to help the Countess dismount. Ilsa Poletska proffered joyful air-kisses to the trainer who abetted her equestrian charade and to his wife who abetted a charade of her own, and then ostentatiously felt for her million-dollar earrings as she bowed to her idolizing throng. The orchestra struck up a rousing rendition of *If You Ever Leave Me* as the handsome and famous neurosurgeon, Dr. Spundrich, friend of presidents, prime ministers, dictators and kings, assisted her over the cavaletti barrier and whisked her to the dance floor. Trey and Jennifer held Bijou and smiled while the crowd milled around his paddock and told him how beautiful he was.

Trey and Jennifer began to realize that their only purpose for being at the gala was to accommodate Bijou. Trey held the Champion's lead line while Jennifer explained to people that their fingers could get bitten off if they didn't present carrot bits to Bijou in the palms of their hands. "Like this," she would demonstrate to the socialites, and then watch Bijou slobber over their manicures as they held the carrot up to his mouth and giggled in his face.

After about two hours, Bijou got bored, raised his tail, and defecated. The crowd politely and quickly meandered away from this sudden polluting of paddock ambience. Trey handed the lead line to Jennifer, walked down the sawdust trail to the side entrance and retrieved a new muck bucket from the van's tack compartment. Gonzalo, the groom who was not allowed into the gala inner sanctum, handed a muck rake to Trey, smirked, and went back to snoozing. Trey deftly scooped the enormous plop into the bucket, carried it back out to the van, and returned to the Champion's paddock without getting a speck of dust on his tuxedo.

"I've had about enough of this, Trey," Jennifer said as she handed Bijou's lead line to her colleague. "I'm going over to the buffet table and get us some lobster salad and a couple of Margaritas. I can't believe that not one person has come over here to even offer us a drink. What's with Ilsa, anyway? She's treating us very shabbily."

As Jennifer lifted her flowered dress and skirts and stepped over the cavaletti poles, Always Cope arrived at the little paddock. "Hey, Trey," he shouted over the music. "Give me that horse and you go with Jennifer to the buffet." He smiled and took the lead line from his assistant. Two teenage girls in formal gowns immediately sidled up to Always to pet his horse and bask in his handsome smile.

"Lordy, Trey, will you look at this food!" Jennifer exclaimed as she scanned the buffet tables. "There is three times more stuff here than all these people can eat! Check out these lobsters!" Jennifer began to pile lobster and shrimp onto her plate while Trey went for the roast beef. "I'm going to get some extra for Gonzalo, Trey. Do you have a pocket in that tuxedo?" Jennifer looked up into the unsmiling face of Countess Poletska.

"Yennifer, Trey!" she said haughtily. "Yoo are not zuppozed to be here! If yoo vant somesing to eat, go to the kitchen and ask somevon zere to find a place for yoo. Zis table of food is reserved for za sponsors of zis sharity! But yoo must hurry back to Bijou, because Alvays doesn't haf time to stand around mit him like zat."

"Ilsa, you invited us to this party," Jennifer said with dismay. "Trey and I aren't servants! We work with Always. We've stayed with Bijou all night as a favor to you, but we haven't had anything to eat or drink since we got here, and it's my birthday! We though we were your friends."

"Yoo haf misunderstood your positions, I'm afraid. Please don't make a scene. Maybe it voould be best if yoo yust vent back over mit Bijou, yah? And I am Countess Poletska, Yennifer. Yoo haf no right to address me as Ilsa. Yoo young peoples must learn your place!"

Jennifer was devastated and Trey was suddenly angry. "I think it's time for us to go," the assistant trainer said to his friend as he sat his plate of food down on the table. "Let's go get Bijou and get out of here."

"Yoo can't yust take Bijou out of here," the Countess retorted. "Ve haven't had our *grand finale* yet!"

"If you want to take Bijou home in your Rolls, then that's up to you," Trey countered. "Otherwise you'd better go kiss him goodnight right now because we, and the groom, and the van, are leaving." He took Jennifer by the arm and headed for Bijou's enclosure.

The Countess hoisted her formal skirts and petticoats with both hands and trundled after them. The fiery indignation in her eyes nearly equaled the brilliance of the giant diamonds dangling from her ears. "Alvays! Alvays! Pleeeze don't let zem take Bijou home now. Zey haven't played *Dancing Queen* for me yet!"

Dr. Spundrich reappeared at the perfect moment to place his hands about the Countess's lithe waist and lift her back over the fence into the paddock. She nearly fell into Always Cope's arms, and her head bumped against Bijou's nose. Bijou's mouth reflexively opened, and the diamond earring from her left ear slid into it. Bijou gulped and swallowed, and the Countess screamed.

"My God! That son of a bitch just swallowed my diamond earring!" she shouted with palpable absence of both accent and gentility. "Always! Reach in there and get that damned rock back!"

Always Cope blinked his eyes in amazement at the cultural transformation of his royal customer. Dr. Spundrich and the other perfect beings in earshot shuddered and stepped away from the paddock fence. Trey and Jennifer first did double takes; then they grinned.

"It's already in his stomach, Ilsa. My arm ain't that long," Cope said with a bewildered look on his face.

"Well gag him, dammit! Make him puke it up!"

"Horses don't vomit, Ilsa. It's going to have to go on through him."

"What! That's ridiculous, you incompetent troll! I can't wait around for half a million dollars worth of diamonds to slide through a stupid horse's bowels!" The Countess reached up with her right hand and slipped off the earring on that side. She held the jewel up in front of her face in the palm of her hand to assure its presence. "Thank God he didn't get this one, too."

At that precise moment, Bijou reached over and slurped the other diamond earring out of her palm. The crowd suddenly became deathly quiet. The Countess lifted both hands to cover her now-naked ears and shouted a yodel-like scream that startled Bijou, who jumped backwards and knocked over the pole fence. The rolling cavaletti poles in turn knocked over several of the luminaria bags, which instantly caught fire. Trey grabbed Bijou's lead line, pulled him forward away from the fire before his flowing tail could ignite, and quickly lead the agitated horse down the shavings-covered path to the exit and the waiting van.

Someone found a fire extinguisher just in time to spray the Countess, whose flowing gown had trailed over one of the luminaria sacks and had begun to smolder. Other guests stomped on the flaming sacks to put out the fires. The Grand Chose Charity Gala came to an ignominious close as Ilsa Poletska, soaked with fire retardant, ran out to her Rolls to follow the van back to the stable where she hoped to recover her million dollars worth of hopefully indigestible assets. Of course, the paparazzi had their cameras flashing to record this unexpected and sensational grand finale.

***

Always Cope had stayed all night with Bijou to retrieve any treasure-laden horse plops that the champion might have chosen to discharge. Ilsa Poletska went home to change clothes and reappeared at Fairy Ring Stables at about nine in the morning just as Dr. McElhern, the veterinarian, arrived. The distraught Countess persuaded the vet to X-ray Bijou's abdomen to confirm the presence and exact location of the jewels.

"There they are," Dr. McElhern said as he pointed to the faceted stones' images on the large film negatives. "My guess is they'll pass on out in twenty-four to thirty-six hours. You'll want to retrieve the manure piles as quickly as you can so the horse doesn't step on the diamonds and break them."

The Countess shook her head angrily. "I can't vait zat long," she blurted with her recovered accent. "Zeese diamonds collateralize my restaurant, and ze bank vants zem back in zere wault today! Put him to sleep and cut zem out of him right now!"

Dr. McElhern squinted and shuddered. "I'll do no such thing, Madam! This horse will pass those stones naturally. It would be inhumane to put him through a surgical ordeal that is totally unnecessary."

"But vhat about me," she retorted testily. "My entire fortune is at risk here. Zose diamonds are all I haf left from my inheritance."

"You sift the plops that this horse passes and you'll have your jewels none-the-worse-for-wear by tomorrow night, maybe even sooner," the vet said sternly. "Neither you, nor anybody else, will make a hole in this animal. Now, you pull up a chair, a shovel, and a bucket and get to waiting."

Frustrated, her accent disappeared again as she glared at Always Cope. "Well, that would be your job then, wouldn't it, Mr. Cope? Or one of the grooms!"

"I didn't get one minute of sleep last night," Always Cope answered as he began to gather the studs from his formal shirt. "This old '*troll*,' as you referred to me last night, is going home to bed now. And I don't think I'd leave the search for those diamonds to minimum wage employees whom you've treated like dirt, Ilsa. You'd better sit here and do it yourself." The tired trainer, now with shirttail hanging out over his tuxedo, shrugged and ambled off toward his house without saying another word.

The Countess picked up a stool and bucket and stomped into the stall where Bijou was lazily chewing alfalfa. She slammed the stall door angrily and sat down in the corner farthest from Bijou's giant dappled rump. The ammoniacal smell of horse urine brought tears to her eyes, and she began to feel very sorry for herself.

"Ah, there you are, Mrs. Beanbot."

Startled, Ilsa Poletska looked up through the bars of the stall door to see who had spoken to her. He was an elderly man in a dark pinstriped suit, whom she recognized as Mr. Skiddoo, her banker. He was the last person on earth that she expected to see on this unhappy Sunday morning.

"Please don't call me that, Mr. Skiddoo. I'm known as Countess Poletska here."

"Not for long, I'm afraid," he answered. "Have you seen the morning papers?" He held the newspaper up so she could see the headline: "CINDERELLA EXPOSED BY HUNGRY HORSE"

The agony of one's undoing suddenly manifested on her face. "Oh God, no! Give me that!" She grabbed for the newspaper through the stall bars and jerked it from the startled banker's hands.

The entire front page consisted of pictures from the Charity Gala. There was a full-faced shot of Ilsa screaming, and her eyes were bigger that Bijou's, who was reacting in the background; her hair and his mane were both extended as if charged by lightning. There was a shot of Ilsa being squirted with a fire extinguisher, a picture of celebrities furtively stamping out luminaria fires, and an unflattering shot of Ilsa running, with the back of her dress charred and gapping, toward the exit after Bijou. Even worse, a nosy reporter had dug up the Countess's past history, and revealed to the sensation-loving public that the popular royal restaurateur was no more related to a Polish Queen than Bijou was. Ilsa Poletska had been born Cassie Sue Condit in Rye, Texas, and there on the front page was her high school graduation picture with a beehive hairdo! The reporter revealed that Cassie Sue was the fifth and last wife of the late Boyce Beanbot, who had been an eccentric oil millionaire, and she'd signed a prenuptial agreement that excluded her from his estate when he died. The wealthy Countess was really a disenfranchised gold-digger who owned a restaurant that she had mortgaged her mansion and her famous earrings to buy, and now her charade was revealed to her once-adoring public.

Ilsa threw open the stall door and began to bawl uncermoniously as Mr. Skiddoo patted her on the shoulder.

"You really must get control of yourself, Mrs. Beanbot. You've got to get me those diamonds back, because they are collateral for your loan, and the bank let you wear them to the charity ball as a favor to you. They are not insured, you know, so we must get them back into the vault today."

"They're inside that stupid horse, you old fool! Why do you think I'd be sitting in that smelly stall if I had them in hand? They'll be out in a few hours, and then you can have them. Now get the hell away from me. I'll call you to come and get the jewels when Bijou passes them." She turned to go back into the stall and screamed again, because Bijou wasn't there.

The distraught Countess and the banker had turned their backs to the stall while they were leafing through the newspaper, and the ever-enterprising Bijou had nudged the door open with his nose and walked quietly out of the barn. Behind the barn he found an open exercise paddock, so he walked in to graze on some inviting greenery. Other horses had recently defecated in the paddock, and Bijou didn't resist the urge to do the same.

Jennifer heard bleating cries from Ilsa and came running to the paddock. She threw a halter on Bijou and took him back to his stall while the horrified owner stared at the manure piles in the paddock and continued to sob. Mr. Skiddoo made a hasty retreat to his car and left the premises wondering why everybody was so upset.

"Which pile did he make?" Ilsa sobbed. "I didn't see which pile Bijou made. Oh Jennifer, what are we going to do now?"

"We," Jennifer answered, "are going to get a big muck bucket and pick up every fresh pile of manure out there. And then you, Ilsa, are going to find a way to sift through it to find your stupid earrings."

Both women got shovels and, assisted by Trey and Gonzalo, proceeded to nearly fill the large plastic container.

Gonzalo couldn't suppress a grin. "You got forty or fifty pounds of *caca* here, Señorita. Where you want me to put it?"

"Put it in the trunk of my car," Ilsa said tersely. "I have a large colander at my restaurant. I'll get my kitchen help to sift it."

"I have a better idea, Ilsa. Why don't you..."

"I don't need any advice from you, Jennifer. Shut your mouth and leave me alone. And if you call me Ilsa again I'll have your job!" The Countess quickly stomped over to her Rolls and opened the trunk for Gonzalo to stuff the huge plastic bucket into it, then got into the car and sped off in a cloud of dust.

Gonzalo was still grinning. "Why didn't she take the bucket to Dr. McElhern's clinic and get it X-rayed? I bet those diamonds are still in Bijou and not in that bucket."

"That's what I was trying to tell that dimwitted egocentric witch," Jennifer said coolly.

***

Ilsa Poletska parked her Rolls Royce behind her restaurant near the entrance to the kitchen and went inside to fetch a couple of the dishwashers to help her unload the manure bucket. She found the largest colander in the equipment pantry and placed it in a large sink. "Pour that stuff in here," she instructed, "and flush it with lots of water. Get some big spoons and stir it so it'll flow through the colander." Her face was contorted from the offensive odor of the equine excrement.

Just as the sifting process started, Pierre, who was the restaurant's Cordon Bleu chef, walked into the kitchen from the dining area. "Mon Dieu! Merde! Ilsa, what are you doing to my keeetchen! You can't do that! Not today!" Pierre's face displayed a hue of purple that hinted of imminent fatality.

"Shut up, Pierre! This is my restaurant and I'll do what I want with it. Turn that water on faster, boys, the sink is plugging up. Turn on the disposal and force that dirty water on out."

Pierre didn't shut up. "Ilsa, the inspectors are coming any minute! You won't have a restaurant if they find a bucket of merde in the keeetchen!"

"Whut? Whut! Oh no! Pierre, why didn't you tell me!"

At that precise moment, two City Sanitation Department agents wandered into the kitchen. Their eyes got bigger than saucers when they smelled horse manure and then caught sight of it splashing all over the preparation tables. Ilsa dropped her giant spatula into the bucket and headed for the exit.

"You'd better run, Lady, because this place is closed indefinitely as of this minute," one inspector shouted as she ran to her car. "I'll leave the citation right here by your bucket of excrement!"

That evening Gonzalo saw something shiny in the bedding of Bijou's stall, and he found both earrings grubby but intact. He washed them carefully, put them in a Baggie, and called Always Cope to come and retrieve them for the Countess. Dr. McElhern had been right; the Beanbot jewels were none-the-worse-for-wear.

The Countess, however, was irreparably frazzled.

***

Late the next morning Jennifer stood reading a newspaper by the Fairy Ring Stable entrance. The headlines stated that social maven and Beanbot heiress Ilsa Poletska had received notice of closure of her upscale restaurant for sanitation violations.

"Restaurant customers with weak hearts had best not read the contents of the citation," the reporter warned.

A car came onto the grounds and discharged the pinstriped person of Mr. Skiddoo, who walked directly to Jennifer.

"The Countess isn't here this morning," Jennifer said as he approached. "She picked up her diamonds from Mr. Cope and then told him to sell her horses. I guess the closing of her restaurant was the crowning blow to her charade."

"I didn't come here to see Mrs. Beanbot, Madam. Aren't you Jennifer?"

"Yes, Sir. Uh, what do you want with me?"

"You are an orphan, and you turned twenty on Saturday. Is that right?"

"Yes. So what?"

"Do you know who John Q. Streicher is?"

"Oh, that's old Uncle John. He was my mother's brother. I met him when I was little. He was kind of a recluse, but a pretty neat old guy. He lived in a barn and taught me how to ride horses. I never saw him after my mother died when I was ten. He never tried to help me or even contact me, so I guess I forgot about him."

"Well, he didn't forget about you, Jennifer. He just passed away and left you about thirty million dollars that he'd made in a telecommunications venture. My bank is the trustee, and it's my job to see that you get every penny of it."

Jennifer's knees weakened from surprise and she steadied herself on Mr. Skiddoo's arm. "Do you mean, Sir, that I'm rich enough to have anything I want?"

Mr. Skiddoo smiled and turned to walk with the tall pretty girl into the barn. "Just about anything, Madam. Horses like Bijou, for instance. Or restaurants. Oh, do you like diamonds? I know where you can find some spectacular earrings at a bargain price!"

THE CATCHCOLT

Horses often live into their thirties, and they deserve to spend their last years in comfort after toiling on the racetrack or in the show ring. Broodmares are particularly deserving because of the risks they take during gestation and foaling. So I bought a special ranch in West Texas and brought my retired horses here to live out their sunset years in spacious green pastures. I'm pretty old, so I moved here with them, and that's why you get to read this tale.

The place had been used for hunting game at one time, and the previous owner had surrounded it by high-fence that only the smallest rabbits could get through. The few deer that were inside the fence were fat from the lush grass and plentiful acorns that was available to them without competition from interloping deer, elk, and feral pigs that roamed the rest of the countryside for a hundred miles in any direction. I blocked off two sixty-acre paddocks on either side of a shallow creek in a flat area that extended south to a rolling mountain range, erected large loafing sheds on the north sides of both enclosures, and turned a half-dozen old mares into one field and a few retired geldings into the other.

They all thought they had gone to heaven. The alpha mare in the distaff paddock was The Queens Mittens. Queenie, as we called her, had been a multiple stakes winning Thoroughbred racehorse before producing twelve spectacular foals in her second and long career as a broodmare. She'd had some difficulty with the last delivery, so rather than risk her life with a thirteenth breeding she was pensioned to the West Texas easy living, which she richly deserved. She was the queen of the mares' paddock, and the other girls showed her grudging equine respect. At age twenty-six she could outrun all of them, and that included a stray deer or two that sometimes got caught up in the horseplay. Queenie loved apples, and Jose, the ranch foreman, brought apples and carrots to all of the horses every day. The other horses always waited their turn while Jose fished the first apple out of his bucket for Queenie.

Then one year a drought ravished the West Texas countryside. The creeks dried up, and the lushness turned to rocky soil and brown thistle-infested dead grass. For six months during the summer and fall we brought hay to the sheds to supplement the skimpy forage. The heat was unbearable, even into October, and Jose and I would go out to the paddocks with garden hoses and cool the old folks down. The horses started to look thin in spite of our efforts, because they were so miserable from the heat and dust that they didn't care much about eating.

Everyone in West Texas prayed for rain, but it didn't come, and the human population suffered, too. My back ached from tossing hay bales, and Jose had a bad knee that caused him to grimace with every step. Jose's seven-year-old daughter, Mary Jane, had asthma and allergies that required frequent trips into town to the doctor, and we spent a lot of time teaching her school lessons that she had missed. I was beginning to think about closing the ranch down for the winter and transporting the horses to East Texas where they could be more easily managed. But then, in the last hot dry week of October, a sudden and strange change in the weather occurred. This started an incredible chain of events that would last sixteen months, and you probably won't even believe it.

Mary Jane was just getting off the school bus on a Friday afternoon when lightning flashes began to snake across the darkening sky. An icy wind joined the thunderous reports to herald the coming winter's first "norther." Texans are used to northers, and always anticipate the first one with time-honored appreciation of the way God changes the seasons here. But this norther was late, was unpredicted by the Weather Service, and was uniquely different. The wind was clean, and so was the moisture in it. As Mary Jane ran wheezing to her father's quarters, sleet and rain captured dust and grime from the air and brought it to ground. The little girl arrived home after a brisk run in the rain and wasn't out of breath.

"Papi, Papi!" she exclaimed to Jose. "It's raining, Papi, and the air is getting clean and I can breath! Let's go out to the sheds and make sure the horses are safe from the lightning!"

Jose was delighted to see his child shouting excitedly without being short of breath, but he had reservations about running outside through a lightning storm. He gave her a welcome-home hug, but made no move toward the door.

"Come on, Papi! You haven't taken any apples to Queenie yet! Lets take some apples out and be sure they're all safe from the storm." Mary Jane grabbed a little yellow slicker and a big one from a peg in the mudroom, and threw the larger one to her dad. The rainproof garments were dusty and stiff from six months of non-use. "It's a special day, Papi! It's raining! Come on!"

Jose couldn't remember a time that Queenie wasn't first in line for an apple. He stood under the metal roof of the loafing shed with rain pelting down vigorously and wondered aloud where she might be. He cupped his hands over his forehead as he focused on the distant trees where the flatland met the mountain to the south, but he couldn't get a glimpse of the old mare.

"I don't see Queenie, Mary Jane, do you?"

"No, Papi, I don't see her. But Queenie's very wise, Papi. I bet she's in the trees getting out of the rain. There isn't any lightning striking now, Papi, so she's probably alright, don't you think?"

Jose knew that lightning was deadly for horses, but he saw no reason to belabor the point. "Let's go home to bed, Mary Jane. I think you're right, and she's okay. We'll just have to see about her tomorrow."

The next morning was glorious with sunshine, warmer breezes, and the pristine aura of cleanliness brought on by the first rain in over six months. The drought was broken, and within the span of a day green sprouts were emerging in the long-seared paddocks. The norther had not brought tornados or crippling ice, but instead had blessed our little valley with prayed-for relief. Queenie, seemingly unruffled by the previous night's events, came down to the loafing shed for her daily apple, and everything seemed right with the world.

Rain came again three days later. The total precipitation was about an inch over a period of sixteen hours. There was no sleet, no flooding, and no violent wind. This precipitation pattern occurred regularly, and by Christmas, there had been a repeated rainstorm every three or four days, but never an ice storm or flood. All of the horses grew coats of winter hair and began to put on weight from eating the winter grass that issued forth from the regularly wetted turf.

My back stopped hurting and Jose didn't limp as much. Mary Jane stopped itching and wheezing entirely and began to grow like a weed. It seemed that a miraculous season had befallen us, and yet we were blithely unaware that many surrounding regions of West Texas were still experiencing inclement weather and unanswered prayers.

Winter passed as though it had been an early spring, and the spring-like weather continued through the summer. Our trees were laden with peaches and plums and acorns, and the Bermuda grass was high enough to tickle the horses' bellies. Jose commented that the horses were so fat they looked pregnant, and we realized that we were truly blessed. The intermittent rain continued throughout the summer months, and the temperature never went over one hundred degrees for the first time in over a century. It was as if Ceres and Proserpina had conspired with The God We Know to replicate Heaven on Earth. Fall simply did not come to pass as the idyllic season carried past August, but in late September an event did occur that got our rapt attention.

I was sleeping on a Sunday morning during that moment in time when the world lights up but the sun has not yet cleared the horizon. Yogi, my aptly named dog who was half poodle, half cocker spaniel, and half mutt, jumped off the bed and ran barking to the back door. I threw on a robe and opened the door expecting to see Jose but was greeted by an excited Mary Jane.

"Papi says to come to the mares' shed quick, Mr. Boss!" she shouted. "We have a new baby!"

"A baby? What kind of a baby?" I asked, still stupid from sleeping.

Mary Jane looked at me like I was daft. "A horse baby, Mr. Boss! Queenie had him last night! Come on, Mr. Boss, you gotta see this new baby!"

I dressed hurriedly, put Yogi and Mary Jane in my pickup, and drove up to the loafing shed by the mares' paddock. Sure enough, there was The Queens Mittens standing there munching one of Jose's apples while a foal happily suckled her breakfast offering.

"What in the hell is that!" I exclaimed. I exclaimed it because the foal was the most amazing animal I'd ever seen in forty years of breeding and racing Thoroughbred racehorses. He was a colt, and he was coal black, except for his scruffy little mane and baby's tail, which were pristine white. He also had a white star high on his forehead where every horse has a cowlick, and a white spot just behind and above each shoulder. His conformation was exquisite, with perfect shoulders and rump, correct legs, and perfectly angled pasterns. He was fearless, and he walked over to nuzzle my hand; he was a foal that you had to love. He was a bloodstock agent's dream-come-true-turned-into-a-nightmare because his sire was unknown and his pedigree, whatever it was, could never be verified.

"How could this possibly have happened?" I said to Jose. "There isn't a stud horse within ten miles of this paddock. This whole farm is completely fenced, and this mare hasn't been off these premises in four years."

"It's a miracle, Mr. Boss," Mary Jane said with a grin.

"Yeah, right," I said as I reached over to pat Queenie on her neck. "What have you gone and done, Fat Lady, and when did you do it?"

Queenie drew up the angles of her mouth as she nuzzled my shoulder. Horses do indeed smile, and Queenie left no doubt in my mind that this genuine smile had an air of mystery about it.

***

Since the colt's mother was The Queens Mittens, little Mary Jane decided to call him Mitty, and the irony of this moniker never occurred to us during the time he lived with us. Mitty thrived, the temperate weather continued, the grass grew, the pain in my back stayed away, Jose stopped limping, and Mary Jane, who played with Mitty every day, was unencumbered by the illnesses that had plagued her infancy. Our horse management enterprise was taking place in an idyllic world, and I was very content.

But I was also compelled to uncover the mystery of Mitty's sire, because it's always an embarrassment for a horsemen to be thought of as lax in protecting his fillies and mares from marauding stallions, particularly stallions with pedestrian pedigrees, or worse, no pedigree at all.

Jose and I mounted our cow-ponies and rode the entire high-fence line. There were no breaks or collapses to be found. We didn't find a foot of fence that even a midget horse could have crawled under. We talked with neighbors and farmhands, and concluded that no one could possibly have brought a stud horse onto the premises during the previous October. We did recall that the drought-relieving rainstorm had occurred exactly three hundred and thirty-nine days before Mitty was born, and Jose remembered that Queenie hadn't come down to the shed that night. But there was absolutely no way that she could have escaped the paddock and then crossed over the high-fence to find a wandering stud.

I had lunch with our equine veterinarian, Dr. Winterstahl, and told him the whole story. "It's simple enough," he responded. "We'll draw DNA studies on the foal, and after the sire is implicated, you can figure out how he got to your mare. You know, a disgruntled farmhand could even have artificially inseminated her."

"I don't have any disgruntled farmhands, and even if I did, how could an uneducated laborer who's never seen an artificial insemination in his life obtain a specimen and introduce it into Queenie out under the trees in a rainstorm?"

"You've got a point there," Dr. Winterstahl allowed. "So it'll take me two or three weeks to get results, and then we can decide how it happened after we get a lead on the bloodlines."

***

I had put Queenie and Mitty in a large paddock all to themselves so they could run about safely, and Mitty would gambol in circles around his mother as she galloped across the field. Mitty's conformation became even more beautiful with each passing week as he grew with vigor, The spring-like weather, which was conducive to great foal development, continued through the entire month of October, and it seemed that we were going to experience another mild winter.

When he was five weeks old, it occurred to me that I hadn't heard from Dr. Winterstahl about the DNA reports. The colt's tests were very important because they might reveal enough information to get Mitty some sort of pedigree, which would enhance his value. So I called the vet for his findings.

"We didn't even have a remote match to any Thoroughbred bloodlines," the doctor said solemnly. "So I had the samples matched with the Quarter Horse registry, and I got nothing there either. Then I tried Paint Horses and Palominos, the Paso Finos, Standardbreds and Walking Horses, Clydesdales, Percherons, Irish and every other kind of Warmblood, and even Przewalski ponies and donkeys and zebras! Your foal is equine, but he isn't related to any horse species on earth that has been typed for DNA! You've got over two thousand bucks invested in these studies; how much more do you want to spend?"

"Well, at least he isn't a mule," I said dejectedly. "So where do I go from here that isn't a waste of money?"

"Maybe you have some kind of spontaneous foal combustion," Dr. Winterstahl said encouragingly. "Why don't you consult with a geneticist? I can give you a reference at the University."

Within minutes I found myself talking with Dr. Coiling from the University of Texas, who claimed to know just about everything that had ever been deducted from looking at chromosomes through an electron microscope.

"What is the sex of that fetus?" the eminent scientist queried when I asked him if there was the slightest possibility that this foal was the result of a spontaneous gestation.

"He's not a fetus," I replied. "He's a living baby horse who is running around on my farm very much alive and lab-confirmed as a genetic male."

"Spontaneous gestations don't occur in chordates, but even if they could it wouldn't result in a male offspring, because there aren't any Y chromosomes in a female ovum. If meiosis-gone-awry resulted in the development of an embryo, it certainly would not be..."

I hung up the phone, because meiosis and embry-whatever fog my brain. I was stuck with the most perfectly conformed horse that had ever trod earthen firmament, and he was of no value whatsoever as a potential racehorse. "Shit," I said to myself, "when he grows up I'll teach him how to fly. Maybe I can sell him to a circus!" I shouldn't have thought that.

***

The strange spring season that had begun during a bizarre October thunderstorm sixteen months before continued directly into the newest calendar spring that was designated to begin in April. Mitty was now six months old, he was as tall as his mother, and he was beginning to take on the habitus of an adult. Which meant that I was due for some new surprises.

RD Weilburg

The magnificent white star on his forehead began to bulge. At first I thought Mitty had bumped his head on a fence or a feed bucket, but the swelling persisted and he began to rub it on fence posts and trees and even with his front feet. I didn't call Dr. Winterstahl because his clinic was forty miles from my front gate, but I got out my digital camera and took pictures of the bulging star on my otherwise perfect equine specimen. A few days, and a few snapshots, went by when it occurred to me that Mitty was growing a horn! I ran to my computer with my camera and downloaded the snapshots.

The computer responded dramatically and succinctly: *"You have attempted an illegal download and this program is shutting down".* I rebooted my computer and tried again. *"The files you are attempting to download have been deleted. You must recreate the file."* I plugged the digital camera back into the computer and restarted the program again. *"No files are available to download because your cache is empty. You may download any pictures that you subsequently take. Enjoy your photographic experience!"*

I drove back up to the paddock and took another good look at my blossoming boy. A well-formed spiral white horn was now protruding from his forehead, and there was no doubt in my mind that the horse we had named Mitty was a unicorn! Once more I pulled out the camera, and I had taken a couple of snaps when I noticed that the white spots on Mitty's shoulders were starting to bulge. And then, before my very eyes, Mitty began to grow wings, huge white-feathered wings that extended ten feet from his coal-black body when he stretched them out, and he whinnied proudly as he displayed them for me. Mitty had morphed into a unicorned Pegasus, and I had him on my camera! I gave Queenie and Mitty a whole bucketful of apples and sped my pickup back to the house. On the way, more amazing things happened. Snow began to fall, and by the time I got to the house visibility was zero, and the power had gone off. I slogged through the rapidly falling snow and went into the darkened house through the back door. As I sat my camera on the kitchen counter, a thunderbolt shook the windows, and lightning lit the house and yard like Klieg lights welcoming a magnificent event. I recoiled as the camera exploded into flames and fizzled away into a smoldering glob. The night had become dark, cold and eerily silent. I lit a candle, sat down on a barstool, poured myself a brandy, and wondered if anybody would ever believe this.

The next morning Yogi barked in my ear to inform me that Jose was at the door. The foreman had come to check on me because the power had not yet been restored, and it was cold both outside and inside. Never, he commented, had there been a snowfall in April in this part of Texas. Mary Jane, warmly dressed, was with him because the school bus wouldn't be coming by after an unanticipated snowstorm. We decided to walk to the paddocks and see how Queenie and Mitty were doing.

We saw two sets of tracks in the snow heading south toward the trees, and were surprised to find that Queenie wasn't responsible for either set because she was standing in the shed nibbling hay. She looked back toward the mountain as we walked up, and there was a faraway look in her brown eyes.

"Mitty has gone away with his daddy," I said to Mary Jane. "I don't want you to be upset. He was a very special horse and had a very special mission here with us."

"I understand," Mary Jane said with a slight wheeze. "But he'll be back someday, I just know. Queenie will miss him, too."

RD Weilburg

    Jose limped over to Queenie and gave her an apple slice. The cold made my back hurt, but I reached up to Queenie and patted her on the neck. Because she was munching the apple, I couldn't really tell if she was smiling, but I think she was.

REGGIE'S REGIMENT

Reggie Ridgewood never renewed his trainer's license for more than a year, because he was never sure that he would live any longer than that. The one thing he knew for sure was that he'd rather die at the racetrack than in a nursing home, so he acquitted himself in a spry and jovial fashion in order to stem any thoughts that his children might have about putting him away. For sixty years he had worked as a hot-walker, groom, gateman, and assistant trainer for enough responsible employers that he had earned a substantial Social Security stipend. He lived with his favorite granddaughter, Lana, who was a pretty good horse trainer in her own right because she had the good sense to tap his six decades of track wisdom. He met her for dinner at the horsemen's cafeteria almost every evening before the first race started to discuss their favorite subject, which was, of course, racehorses.

"Lana, who is this maiden three-year-old colt named Gonzo Bongo that you're running in the second race for Mike McHenry?" Reggie asked as he shook his head and frowned. "What idiot would embarrass an innocent horse with such a ridiculous name?"

Lana giggled. "Mike bought him at some county fair meet in Wyoming. He's had four races and has never finished ahead of another horse. Since he's already raced, Mike couldn't change his name. He bought his full brother, too, who's a two-year-old-in-training."

Reggie continued to frown. "Why on earth would he buy a colt that can't beat the next-to-the-worst runner in Wyoming and bring him here to Texas to run with our best? And buy another one just like him? Mike musta had a dumb attack. A *double* dumb attack!"

"Mike didn't think the colt had been conditioned well enough to race. He thought that with a little time, I could do it. I think I have, Grampa. You'll notice that he's going off at ninety-to-one. Might be a good bet."

"Do you mean you think he can win it?"

"No," Lana answered frankly. "The morning-line favorite in that race, Rackin Roger, is going to go gate-to-wire. Gonzo just won't be able to pass him, unless we get very lucky. Bet him to show, Grampa. At these odds you'll make some money."

Reggie had just made a quarterly payment on his Medicare supplemental insurance, and he only had twenty dollars left from his Social Security check after paying for dinner. He studied the racing program for a few more minutes to assess the track handicapper's morning line, and realized that the second and third favorites were closers that had both been second by a neck in their previous races. Reggie suddenly had a *superfectal* thought!

"I'm going to bet Gonzo Bongo behind Rackin Roger and ahead of the seven and eight horses for the superfecta!" Reggie announced with a grin.

"Oh Grampa! You know that the odds are really stacked against you to pick four horses in order, especially if one of your picks is going off at ninety-to-one. You're gonna loose your two bucks, you silly old goat."

Ten Horse Tales

Reggie smiled confidently. "You go over to the saddling barn and do your job, Honey. You leave the betting to your old Grampa. I'll see you after the race."

Reggie walked over to the grandstand and took the escalator to the second floor, where he promptly ensconced himself at his favorite bar and ordered a large iced tea.

The blonde barmaid was called Whimsy Lee, and every one at the track knew that Whimsy's mother had had a stroke of genius when she selected her daughter's name.

"No bourbon tonight, Mr. Reggie?" she purred.

"I wouldn't have enough money left for a tip if I was drinkin' hard stuff," he said candidly as he passed her an extra dollar. "Wet me down with tea so I can go make a daring wager!" He gulped the tea and went over to the pari-mutuel window to place his bet with all the money he had left.

Reggie's heart nearly stopped as he watched Rackin Roger hold off Gonzo Bongo by a head, and the seven and eight horses crossed the wire in that order just behind. The latter two had closed fast, but not fast enough to catch the front-runners, and Reggie Ridgewood stood openmouthed as he realized that he had, indeed, won the superfecta!

Reggie's hands were trembling as the pari-mutuel teller handed him a check for over eight thousand dollars, which represented his winnings after Uncle Sam had extracted twenty per cent for income tax. The elderly horseman then headed to the escalator, which would take him down to the track level where his granddaughter would be waiting to find out if he had picked a winner. And that is when Reggie Ridgewood's luck took a life-changing plunge.

Reggie stepped on a carelessly discarded ice cube and fell head first down the escalator. He landed in a contorted heap at the bottom, where he struggled to see if the check for his winnings was still in his fist. A crowd of racing spectators came running to his aid.

"I think I've broken my hip," the crumpled old man groaned as pain began to register. Then he looked up to smile at his fellow handicappers. "But I picked the superfecta, by golly!"

***

On the fifth day after hip replacement surgery, Reggie sat on his bed waiting for his doctor to come around to release him from the hospital. Lara sat beside him, and she wasn't smiling.

"Grampa," the pretty young horse trainer said in a serious tone, "you can't come home, because I have to be at the track at five every morning and there isn't anybody else to look after you. I've made arrangements for you to go to the Papillon Extended Care Facility until you have recovered enough to take care of yourself. I'm sorry, Grampa, but there just isn't any other way to get you rehabilitated."

"Papillon! That's a nursing home, Lara! I'd rather be shot dead than go to a nursing home. Please don't send me away to die, Lara."

"No, Grampa. I wouldn't do that! They have a special unit at Papillon where surgical patients get intermediate care. You know, physical therapy and stuff like that. Your insurance company wants to avail you to this service so you can recover more quickly. I promise that you can come home in a couple of weeks, and then you can come to the track with me every day and be my number-one training advisor, just like always. So, the quicker you get over there and start rehabilitating, the quicker you can get out and get back to the old routine. Okay?"

Reggie grimaced. "Okay, Lara. You're right, of course. I'll go over there with the fogies. I just hope old age isn't contagious."

***

Reggie was wheeled into a double room and assisted into his bed.

"Welcome to Papillon Rehab, Mr. Ridgewood," the smiling nurse said as she beckoned toward an old man in the other bed. "Meet Mr. Greenberg, your roommate. Mr. Greenberg, you be nice to Mr. Ridgewood, now; he's going to be with us here for a couple of weeks."

Mr. Greenberg wore an oxygen mask that made a constant hissing sound because of the high rate of gas that was flowing through it. He grunted a hello that was slightly louder than the oxygen flow. "What crime against health got your body committed to this joint," he uttered to Reggie without looking in his direction.

"I fell down an escalator, hip first. How about you?"

"I married seven women," Mr. Greenberg replied.

"Ah, and they broke your heart," Reggie said, grinning. Reggie couldn't see his roommate's mouth because of the oxygen mask, but he could see a smile in his eyes.

"Chamber by chamber and artery by artery," the wheezing man answered. "The chicksas were bad, but the princesses were the worst! My heart's trashed, my money's gone, and I'll never see Belmont Park again."

Reggie turned and dropped his legs over the edge of his bed to face his new friend. "Belmont, you say? Are you a follower of the ponies? That's what I do for a living."

Mr. Greenberg sat up in bed and lifted the mask from his face as he turned toward Reggie. "Well you don't say! The fates have answered my prayers, and we do indeed need to be friends! You can call me Sam Seventeen. What do I call you, Mr. Ridgewood?"

"I'm Reggie. What the hell does Sam Seventeen mean?"

"I was the seventeenth Samuel Greenberg in the Queens telephone directory. It just stuck on me. Do you have anybody that can get a bet down for me?"

"That I can do, Sam Seventeen. My granddaughter will be coming by to visit every night, and I'm sure she'll obligingly convey your investments to the betting windows. She's a trainer, you know, and can give us a little insight."

"Praise God," Sam Seventeen uttered as he reattached his oxygen source. "I have a reason to live!" The sickly old man dropped his skinny legs over the side of the bed and put his feet onto a little plastic stool that was covered with soft red rubber. He reached for his bathrobe, which was draped over a wheelchair beside the bed, and laboriously inserted himself into it. "This ain't a hospital, Reggie, so if we want to eat, we gotta go to the mess hall. If you can walk, you can push me over there, and we can talk about racehorses and wink at some girls."

***

The cafeteria at Papillon Assisted Nursing Center was surprisingly noisy, considering that every customer in it was old, addled, or crippled. Reggie pushed Sam Seventeen alongside the service line as he slid their single serving tray along in front of the food array, which was spectacularly unappetizing in appearance.

"Do you want salmon steak or pork chops?" the serving lady asked Sam Seventeen.

"Gimme two pork chops, if they're well cooked," the spindly invalid answered as he peered through the glass sneeze guard.

She passed a plate of pork chops under the glass and Reggie placed it on the tray.

"I'd like pork chops, too," Reggie said.

"Ain't no more. Sam got the last one," the server said matter-of-factly.

"Uh, I'll have salmon," Reggie responded as he took the already dished plate from the lady and put it on the tray.

"Be sure to get salad and dessert cake," the serving lady said sternly. "They're good for your bowels."

Reggie looked at her askance. "How can cake be good for your bowels?"

"It's made out of bran cereal," was the annoyed reply.

Reggie dutifully placed two salads and two cake slices on the tray, placed the tray across the armrests of Sam Seventeen's wheelchair, and pushed his new friend toward a table where three ancient women were sitting. He pushed Sam up to the table across from the center lady, and pulled up a chair on Sam's left.

The old lady across from Reggie had short curly bleach-blonde hair with red ribbons scattered throughout it. She wore bright red lipstick, excessive rouge, and sported an oversized black beauty mark on her right cheek. Her wrinkly hands were folded beneath her chin as she mouthed a prayer of thanks over her evening meal. She finished her prayer and smiled politely at Reggie as he adjusted his chair.

"Hi, I'm Reggie," the old horseman said in response to her smile. "This is my first day at Papillon."

"Welcome," she said without changing her smile. "My name is Nettie. I am a disciple of Jesus. Sam Seventeen isn't, you know; he's a gambler and won't be going to Heaven." Nettie pointed at the stone-faced gray-haired women sitting in the middle. "This lady next to me is Clotilde, and that gal next to her is Absinth. Be careful of Absinth, she's a vamp."

Absinth proffered a little hello wave at Reggie. Her hair was gunmetal blue-black and was cut very short, and she wore thick pink makeup and lipstick that perfectly matched her pink blouse. "Hello, Reggie," she said with a contrived high-pitched squeak. "Don't you pay no mind to Nettie! I'm not really a vamp. Nettie's just jealous because I used to have lots of affairs when I was married to all those handsome men. What do you do, Reggie? Are you married?"

"I'm a retired horseman, mending from a broken hip," Reggie answered. "My wife died years ago."

Until this moment the stone-faced lady, Clotilde, had given no indication that she was alive. Her eyes and the corners of her mouth drooped in passivity of expression typical of senility. She interrupted the conversation before Absinth could attempt a cutesy comment to Reggie's response. "I used to ride to the hounds, you know. I cut quite a figure sitting up there on a grand gelding, rampaging across meadows and ravines and fences and coops. We jumped over a tractor once. It was really scary and exhilarating at the same time!"

Reggie studied the lady for a split second before he spoke back to her. He was sure that she was at least a hundred and forty years old. "Did you indeed!" he exclaimed with interest. "Were you in Virginia or the Carolinas?"

"I was right here in Texas, at Etoile, at the Chireno Gravel Pits."

"I didn't know there were foxhunts in Texas," Nettie said.

"Lot's of 'em," Clotilde droned. "But we just chased rabbits at Chireno. I jumped over a tractor once."

"Can you cut this pork chop for me, Nettie?" Sam Seventeen asked as he pushed his plate, knife and fork toward her side of the table. "My arthritis is acting up."

Nettie dutifully took the plate and began to cut the pork chops into tiny pieces. "It would be easier to do this if you were a good Christian who didn't gamble, Sam Seventeen. Can't you see that God wants you to mend your ways?"

"Why didn't you ask me, Sam?" Clotilde grouched. "I don't care if you bet on the horses. I jumped over a tractor on one once, you know."

"You should have been chasing men instead of jumping over tractors after rabbits, Clotilde," Absinth sneered. "If you'd caught a husband you wouldn't be here all by yourself now."

"That wasn't a nice thing to say," Sam Seventeen said to Absinth. "I happen to know that Clotilde had a very fine husband once. She just forgets about it."

Clotilde managed to curl her droopy mouth into a smile. "Yes, I had a husband. His name was Henry. He bought me a fine gelding and I used to ride to the hounds."

Absinth pouted at her rebuke and concentrated on eating her salmon steak.

Nettie passed Sam Seventeen his plate of minced pork chops.

Reggie concentrated on his own meal and wondered when the hell he was going to get out of this place. Then it occurred to him to ask if there was a television set somewhere in Papillon Center; at least he could watch horse racing on television while he was recuperating.

"You bet there is," Sam Seventeen said, eager to refocus the conversation to something he was interested in talking about. "They have an entertainment center here. We can watch the ponies run and your granddaughter can place our bets at the track. Is she coming by tonight?"

"She'll stop by on her way to the track. She doesn't have anybody running until nine o'clock. You got a racing form, Sam?"

"Indeed I do, Reggie. Eat your bran cake and let's head for the rec-room."

"I'm coming, too," Absinth said enthusiastically. "I want to learn to bet on the races! Come on, Nettie and Clotilde, y'all come too."

"Gambling is a sin," Nettie admonished. "I don't approve of it in any form. But I'll come along to see the pretty horses. And I want to meet Reggie's granddaughter."

"I love horses," Clotilde mumbled. "I used to ride a big gelding to the hounds. We jumped over a tractor once."

"You're off your medications, aren't you, Clotilde?" Nettie said snidely.

***

Absinth assumed the pushing duties for Sam Seventeen's wheelchair, and Reggie plodded alongside Clotilde, who used a walker at a very low rate of speed. They arrived at the recreation center and sat down around one of several televisions. Sam Seventeen took charge of the remote and began to search for the racing channel.

Reggie saw his granddaughter, Lana, walk by the rec-room entrance, and he called to her. The pretty redhead, delighted to see that her grandfather wasn't brooding about being at the rehab center, hurried in to give him a hug.

Sam Seventeen's eyes widened when he saw Lana come in. He immediately pulled out his cell phone, pulled down his oxygen mask, pushed number one on his speed dial, and whispered gruffly into the receiver. "Get your butt over here quick." He then clicked the phone closed, stuck it back in his pocket, and smiled broadly at Lana before he re-established his oxygen connection. "It's a pleasure to meet you," he wheezed as

Reggie introduced him to her. "You must be adopted, because you're much too pretty to be related to Reggie."

"He's flattering you because you train horses," Nettie said with a sniff. "He's a gambler and morally corrupt, young lady, so you watch out around him!"

Reggie laughed. "And he wants you to go to the window for him tonight. Sam Seventeen may be a reprobate, but I have to agree with his assessment of your pulchritude"

"I like flattery," Lana said as she patted Sam Seventeen on the shoulder. "So whom do you want me to bet for you? And why?"

"I like Cerebral Rocket to win in the seventh race," the frail old man answered.

Lana's brows arched in surprise. "That colt hasn't finished ahead of anybody in eight races. Why on earth would you bet him to win in tough company?"

"He's at a new track, and his trainer would have shipped him to France for dinner if he didn't think his horse had potential. You put this on his nose for me and watch what happens." Sam Seventeen handed Lana a crumpled twenty-dollar bill. He smiled so broadly that the corners of his mouth extended beyond his oxygen mask.

Lana took the money, but glanced furtively at her grandfather.

Reggie winked and nodded affirmatively. "Here, Honey, put twenty dollars on Cerebral Rocket for me, too. I think old Sam's on to something."

"Me too, me too," Absinth chortled as she rummaged through her purse. "I want twenty on that Rocket Nose, or whatever his name is!" She added her bill to Lana's cache of twenties.

"I want twenty dollars on Nose Rocker, too," Clotilde said, uttering each syllable very precisely. "I used to ride to the hounds." The pallid old lady fumbled through her purse and extracted a roll of money that was larger than her fist. She peeled off a twenty and passed it to Lana. "We jumped over a tractor once," she concluded with a wan smile.

Nettie shook her head in disgust, and all of the little red ribbons jiggled. "Gambling is a mortal sin," she groused. "There will be no bookmakers in the Kingdom of Heaven. It pains me to see you all succumb to the will of the Devil."

"Shush and watch this next race," Sam Seventeen wheezed. "I think this little filly named Tammy Taffeta is going to come from behind and win it. The T.V. guys didn't pick her to win, so let's see how good a handicapper I really am."

On the television screen, the starting gate snapped open and ten young fillies spewed out to the singsong voice of the race caller. Tammy Taffeta was dead last down the backstretch, and Sam Seventeen sucked on his oxygen as the pack of galloping two-year-olds rounded the course toward the final stretch. The old ladies were taking on a blue hue from holding their breaths, and then Tammy Taffeta made her move and passed every tiring competitor as she dashed toward the wire to win by two lengths.

Even Nettie was shrieking with excitement as the bay filly cleared the wire. Reggie and Lana were impressed with Sam Seventeen's call and congratulated him for his pick.

"Wish I'd had a bet down on that trip," Sam said to Lana as he gulped oxygen in the aftermath of his prediction. "Please don't forget to put my money on Cerebral Rocket in the seventh tonight!"

"I'm impressed, Mr. Greenberg," Lana gushed. "You can rest assured I'll place your bet. I think I'll put a couple bucks of my own money on that colt tonight!"

At that moment a redheaded sturdy young man rushed into the recreation room. He wore slacks with a blue blazer and blue necktie. His face was flushed with anxiety.

"Are you alright, Zayde?" he asked, using the Yiddish word for grandfather as he strode over to Sam Seventeen's wheelchair. "Your call sounded desperate!"

"Certainly I'm alright, Ryan," the old man wheezed. "I'm glad you got right over here. There's somebody here I want you to meet."

The young man sighed with relief and looked around the room at the collection of folks that surrounded Sam Seventeen and the television set. When his gaze caught Lana he smiled as he realized what his grandfather was up to. It was a glad smile.

"This is my grandson, Ryan O'Bryan," Sam Greenberg announced with rasping voice. "I want you to meet my new roommate, Reggie Ridgewood, and his granddaughter, Lana. Reggie and Lana are racehorse people, Ryan. We are going to do business together."

Ryan had already met all the old ladies that gathered around his grandfather, and he wanted to hug the old man for calling him over for the opportunity to meet Lana. The business part of the introduction slipped by him as he felt himself consumed by infatuation for the pretty girl, whose hair was as red as his own.

"I'm very pleased to meet you, Ryan," Lana said, smiling radiantly. "But I'm sorry to say that I have to leave for work now. I have races this evening, and I have to go to the betting window for these folks first."

"I'll walk you to your car," Ryan said eagerly as he hurried to follow her out of the room.

An hour later the elderly racing fans cheered Cerebral Rocket across the television screen to his first victory. The odds were twenty to one, so they each made over four hundred dollars on their twenty dollar bets. And the excitement wasn't over. Lana's horse won the ninth race, and they all got to cheer again when Ryan showed up in the winner's circle with Lana to be included in the win picture.

After the ninth race, the old folks trundled back to their rooms with grins on their faces. Reggie was delighted that his granddaughter had won a race, and he was delighted that Sam Seventeen had picked Cerebral Rocket to be a winner. Sam seventeen was delighted that he picked a winner, and he was elated that he had matched his grandson up with a good-looking colleen. Absinth and Clotilde were both delighted with the outcome of their bets, and even Nettie, who didn't believe in gambling, delightfully admitted that she had a good time in the company of the horseracing enthusiasts.

***

Lana came to her grandfather's room the next afternoon to turn over the winnings that she had collected for Reggie and his friends. A smiling Ryan O'Bryan was close by her side.

"You bring me money and a happy grandson," Sam Seventeen said to Lana with a wink. "Such a deal!"

"Lana is teaching me all about horses," Ryan laughed. "Won't be long, Zayde, and I'll be able to pick the winners as well as you do."

"Keep your money in your pocket," the old man wheezed. "You won't have enough money to date this pretty girl if you lose it all trying to outsmart the ponies. You let me and Reggie do the handicapping." He handed Lana a paper with numbers written on it and a wad of greenbacks. "Here's who Reggie and I like in the races tonight. There's enough cash there to cover bets for all of our little gang. I guess you could call us Reggie's Regiment!"

Lana took the notations and the money and shook her head in mock disgust. "If our grampas ever get out of the rehab center they'll go straight to the poorhouse!"

"Look again, Honey," Reggie laughed. "We have a lot left over from last night's winnings. A few more nights like this and we can buy our own string of racehorses!"

"That's a great idea," Sam Seventeen rasped. "Start looking for a fast two-year-old for us, Lana. Maybe that will keep me from dying."

"That's right," Reggie said, nodding his head enthusiastically. "If you have a fast two-year-old in the barn, you'll never die! It's a horseracing fact!"

***

And so a routine developed. Every evening Lana stopped by Papillon Center with more money than she'd left with the day before. She'd distribute the winnings to Reggie's regiment of enthralled elderly racing fans, hug everybody and wish them good luck on the next round of bets, and leave for the race track with Ryan O'Bryan in tow. The Regiment, as they now proudly called themselves, would then file to the recreation room to watch the evening's racing events on television. After the races, they would all toast their handicapping success by drinking Dr. Pepper from champagne glasses. Absinth was convinced that Sam Seventeen and Reggie were geniuses, and she began to fantasize about trapping an eleventh husband. Clotilde's memory improved, and she began to remind people of the color of the tractor that she had vaulted whilst chasing the hounds. Nettie, of course, ranted about the evils of gambling and never participated in the betting, but she reveled in the fun of clinking glasses of non-alcoholic bubbly with her friends; and besides, she was beginning to really like horses.

Reggie and Sam Seventeen were on a roll, and Reggie's sentence in the rehabilitation center was about to terminate. His goal, quite simply, had been to walk out of the place with a healthy hip, a pocketful of well-thought-out winnings, and then spend satisfying final years at the track with his beloved granddaughter. But as his last day at the center approached, he knew that he was going to miss his new friends. Reggie was a lucky man, and a fortuitous situation presented that could cement the camaraderie of his regiment of fellow racing enthusiasts.

On the day before Reggie was to be discharged from Papillon Extended Care and Assisted Living Center, Lana stopped by with some interesting news.

" Mike McHenry's wife has given him an ultimatum, Grampa. He's got to get rid of some of his horses and spend more money on her, or she's going to take all of his non-equine estate and move to Patagonia. He wants to quickly sell that two-year-old colt that's a full brother to Gonzo Bongo, and I can have him for six thousand dollars. He's ready to race, Grampa, and he's even faster than his brother. You won eight thousand on the day you broke your hip, and God only knows how much you've won on this two-week roll, so I was wondering if you'd buy him with me. I'll train him for free, Grampa, if you'll buy him."

A light flashed through Reggie's mind. "Has he been named yet? I ain't gonna buy a horse with a stupid name like Gonzo Bongo."

"No, Grampa. We'd have to name him before he could race.

"Okay, I'll buy him, Lana. But only under one condition; we'll syndicate him with my friends here at the nursing center."

"Oh, Grampa! You'll have to get all of them licensed with the Racing Commission! How will you get all those decrepit old people down to the commission office to get photographed and fingerprinted?"

"We can make it happen, Lana. You get your big Irish boyfriend to meet with us here tomorrow when I'm discharged, and we'll take everybody who wants to be a partner over to the track to get licensed. Trust me, Honey. This is going to be a fun thing!"

***

Before he was discharged from the rehab center, Reggie met with all his friends in the rec room to say goodbye and offer them a deal they couldn't refuse. "I paid six grand for this horse, and he's going to make us a fortune. And because we've become such good friends, you can have ten per cent of him for five hundred dollars apiece. Lana and I will own the rest, and Lana will train him for free, as long as we pay her ten per cent of the earnings. We have to agree on a name for him and get it registered with the Jockey Club fast, because he'll have a race in two weeks. Who wants to own a racehorse?"

"I do! I do!" Clotilde croaked as she dug five one-hundred-dollar bills out of her now-bulging purse. "I had a gelding once before. We jumped over a tractor."

"Count me in, partner!" Absinth giggled as she passed a wad of bills to Reggie. "Will you be taking me to the track?"

Reggie nodded as he accepted the money. "Yes, yes. We'll all take the Papillon Center van to the track to get licenses and then we'll go back together every time we have a race!"

"I'll take ten per cent of this deal," Sam Seventeen wheezed, "but there's no way I can go to the track in the condition I'm in. Put my portion of the ownership in Ryan's name, and he can go get the owner's license."

"That'll work, Sam," Reggie said as he took Sam Seventeen's payment and shook his feeble hand. "Welcome to The Regiment. You've made a good investment. So, fellow owners, what do we want to name this critter?"

"Wait a minute! Don't forget me! I want to buy ten per cent of this horse, too."

Everyone looked at Nettie with total shock.

"You want to buy part of a racehorse, Nettie?" Absinth said with her high-pitched squeak. "What would Jesus say about that?"

"The Lord has no qualms about speculative investment," Nettie answered seriously. "I won't be making any sinful bets. I think we ought to name our horse Regimental Mint, because he's going to make lots of money for us by earning it respectably as a fast-running athlete."

"Reggie's Regiment, Regimental Mint. Sounds good to me," Sam Seventeen grunted. "Welcome to the partnership."

"I like the name Reginald Mint," Clotilde drawled. "It reminds me of green. Mine was green, you know."

"Your horse was green?" Absinth asked with a quizzical frown.

"No, silly! The tractor was green. My horse was purple."

"Regimental Mint it is," Reggie stated. "That's a respectable name and he won't be embarrassed when the race caller shouts it over and over when he's winning

As Lana and Ryan carried his luggage to the car, Reggie Ridgewood stuffed his new partners' money into his pocket and walked out of Papillon Rehabilitation and Assisted Living Center with a relieved grin on his face.

***

Reggie and Lana were back at Papillon the next morning, and they climbed into the Center's van with all the regimental partners except Sam Seventeen, who was too feeble to travel. Ryan O'Bryan came in his grandfather's stead. They were taken to the racetrack and delivered to the door of the Racing Commission office.

Lana assisted the old ladies in filling out their owner's license applications. Each new partner had a check made out for the appropriate fee, because, for security reasons, the Racing Commission won't accept cash. Luckily Nettie and Absinth had brought their passports for proof of identity. Clotilde fumbled through her purse and spilled wads of money all over the counter and floor as she searched for her photo ID. People on both sides of the counter retrieved the errant bills for her. She provided a driver's license, which provoked shuddering on both sides of the counter.

"Certainly I can drive," Clotilde proclaimed proudly. "I'm only eighty-four. I jumped over a tractor once. It was green."

The Commission clerks then assisted everybody in getting their fingerprints recorded by a fancy new inkless machine. By the time Clotilde got all ten fingertips recorded, everyone was very thankful that ink wasn't involved. Then they lined up to get their pictures taken for their identification.

Nettie primped her hair, straightened all of her little red ribbons, and checked her flaming red lipstick with a hand mirror before she placed her toes on the line on the floor and smiled into the camera. The laminated plastic license then issued forth from the camera equipment and the Commission lady attached it to Nettie's collar. Nettie studied it to her satisfaction with her little mirror.

The process was repeated with Absinth, who presented, as usual, slathered in pink lipstick and wearing a pink blouse with a pink glass-beaded necklace. Absinth was followed by Ryan O'Bryan, who was clad smartly, and then Clotilde was last up to the line. Clotilde looked as though she had just emerged from a homeless shelter.

"What does it say there on that little badge?" Clotilde asked as the clerk pinned it to her collar. The picture on the badge looked like a post-mortem mug shot.

"It says 'OWNER,'" the Commission lady answered politely.

"Do I own the racetrack now?" Clotilde said wondrously.

"Fraid not, Honey," the Commission lady said with a surprised look. "But you do own a racehorse." She glanced over to Lana for help.

"You just bought part of Regimental Mint, remember?" Lana said to Clotilde as she carefully enunciated each syllable. "With that badge, you can go over to the backside stables and see him now."

"What a marvelous idea," Clotilde said with an enormous wrinkly grin. "I used to ride to the hounds, you know, on a purple gelding."

Lana, Reggie, and the four newly licensed owners got back into the van and were driven to the backside barn where their colt, Regimental Mint, lived. The new owners flashed their identification badges with pride as they passed uniformed guards into the high-security stabling area.

Lana asked a groom to bring Regimental Mint to the lawn beside the shed row, and the horse stood there while his new owners marveled at his conformation.

"I have a race picked out for him in two weeks," Lana announced. "He's ready to run for you. Come say hello to him."

Clotilde proved that she really did know about horses; she gently walked up to the big quiet bay colt and kissed him on the nose. "You're a sweet boy, Reginald, and there's a kiss for good luck," she cooed. "I expect you to mint me some money real soon.'"

Nettie and Absinth weren't to be outdone, so they went over and kissed the colt on the nose, too. The groom took a picture of all of them standing happily with their new lithe running machine. Regimental Mint was then led back to his stall with red and pink lipstick all over his nose.

***

Two weeks later Reggie and Lana came by the Papillon Center to discuss the pending race with Sam Seventeen. They found the old gambler blue-faced and struggling for every breath. His grandson, Ryan, was at his side.

"My God, Sam," Reggie said. "Do you need to be transferred out of here to a hospital? You don't look so good."

The old man groaned his reply. "You didn't know me before I got sick, Reggie. I really don't look any different. I got an Irish grandson to watch after me, and a fast two-year-old in the barn, which guarantees that I won't be dying anytime soon. So what are our odds tonight."

"They got us pegged at ten-to-one," Reggie answered. "Since it's his first race, I don't think the last-minute bettors are going to bring those odds down. Hell, he could go out there and start looking around and finish last, you know. Which doesn't mean he can't run fast."

Sam Seventeen forgot to take a breath while he was pondering what Reggie had said. He began to cough and turn a shade of purple that was darker than Clotilde's imaginary horse. Ryan turned up the oxygen volume and supported Sam's mask while the old man gasped air from it.

"So many distractions from what's important," Sam Seventeen finally wheezed. "I wish I could go to the track, but I can't. So put a thousand dollars on Regimental Mint's nose for me, Reggie. What's his number."

"Zayde, that's a big part of your nest egg," Ryan warned his grandfather. "Reggie just said that he might not win!"

"Well, then," Sam Seventeen grunted, "I'll bet two thousand on him next time, to make it up. He's fast, you know."

Reggie put Sam's wager in his pocket. "His number is two, Sam. His white silks will be easy to follow on the T.V. screen." He turned to Ryan. "I'll call you when the post parade starts. I wish you could be with us at the track, but we all understand that your grandfather is in no shape to travel tonight. Get those old ladies on the van in time for the race, and I'll meet them at the track and watch after them."

"We'll be back here as soon as I get my chores done after the race," Lana said to Ryan. "Don't let Sam get too excited."

Ryan kissed her on the cheek and smiled. "Good luck," he said as he winked at her. "Bring me a win picture."

***

"Look at all those tractors on the track," Clotilde exclaimed to the other members of Reggie's Regiment. "Are they racing?"

"They're preparing the surface for the next race," Reggie explained. "It has to be really smooth for the horses to run on it safely. Regimental Mint will be running in this race. Let's go over to the paddock and watch them saddle him up."

Reggie and the three ladies made their way to the paddock and stood with the crowd of racing fans to watch Lana saddle their horse. They were in the number-two stall, which corresponded to the pole position in the starting gate and also meant that Regimental Mint would be wearing a white saddle pad, and his jockey would be wearing matching white silks. The jockey's valet brought the officially weighed saddle to Lana, who placed it on Regimental Mint and cinched it deftly. The groom then led the colt out to the circular paddock for the jockey to mount.

"That sure is a little track," Clotilde said as she squinted into the paddock. "Where's the finish line?"

"This is the saddling paddock," Reggie said, somewhat annoyed by the old lady's prattle. "The race will be at that big track we were at a few minutes ago."

Clotilde gave a comprehending nod. "Oh, good. That's a lot bigger. Reginald won't have to jump over any of those tractors, will he? That isn't easy to do, you know. I had to jump over a tractor once."

Nettie rolled her eyes, took Absinth by the arm, and spoke quietly so Clotilde couldn't hear. "That woman is driving me to distraction, Absinth. I am succumbing to an urge to sin. Come over to the betting window with me and show me how to bet on our horse before I start looking for a tractor to run over her with."

Absinth did a double take before smirking haughtily through her pink makeup. "I knew there was some devil in you, Nettie! Follow me to the window, and then follow me to the bar. Bettin' and drinkin' will offend the Lord less than murder!"

Down at the finish line Reggie and Clotilde didn't even notice that Nettie and Absinth were giddily sipping on margaritas. Because the race was a short sprint, the starting gate was on the backstretch, and the horses would take only one turn before charging down the stretch to the finish line.

They all cheered as Regimental Mint was ponied by in the post parade and led around the oval to the backstretch where the race would begin. They waited with bated breath as the big bay colt was loaded into the starting gate, and they felt their hearts jump into their throats when the announcer shouted "They're off and running!"

Regimental Mint stumbled to his knees as he left the gate, and his jockey showed great skill by shifting his balance backward and staying on the colt as the inexperienced horse struggled to regain his footing. The pack of competitors was far ahead when Regimental Mint felt steady enough on his feet to dig in and start running. The colt was trailing the pack by ten lengths when he rounded the turn toward the home stretch, and his jockey pulled him alongside the rail so the distance around the turn would be minimalized. Showing amazing resolve, the colt quickly overtook one horse after another in the stretch, and was beaten by only half a length as he crossed the wire behind the winner of the race.

Reggie and his regiment stood slack-jawed as they realized that they had nearly won the race after a horrific start. Every one of the coterie except Clotilde had bet Regimental Mint to win, and they had all, except for Clotilde, lost their money.

Clotilde had bet the partnership's horse to show, because she was nervous about the tractors being in his way. She had to ask Reggie how to go cash her winning ticket, and she painstakingly packed the winnings into her already bulging purse. "I'm really worried about Sam Seventeen," she said as they boarded the van for the Papillon Center. "He may not realize how fast his horse really is. He needed to win tonight more than I did, you know. He's never jumped over a tractor."

***

Samuel Greenberg and his grandson had watched the race on television and had been privy to only one replay, which hadn't clearly depicted the problem at the starting gate. They regretted not having been at the track to watch repetitive instant replays.

"What do you think, Reggie?" Sam Seventeen wheezed. "Was he as fast as we'd hoped?"

"You're going to live forever," Reggie assured him with a broad grin. "Regimental Mint is the fasted two-year-old I've ever laid eyes on! He fell to his knees, Sam, and still damned near ran over the winner! Wait til next time!"

"I really don't know if I can make it til next time," Sam Seventeen whispered through his oxygen mask. "Tell me again how fast he is."

"You can bet your fortune on his nose next time," Reggie said confidently.

"Grampa's right," Lana chimed in as she slipped her hand into Ryan's. "If he comes out of the gate on his right lead and doesn't bump anybody, he'll win by five lengths, I promise, Mr. Sam."

Absinth leaned down and whispered into Sam Seventeen's ear loudly enough that everyone could hear. "In two more weeks

Regimental Mint's gonna win, we're all gonna get rich, and I'm gonna leave pink all over your face!"

"I'm going to bet on him, too, Sam Seventeen," Nettie said. She jiggled her little red ribbons so Sam could be sure whom it was that was talking to him. "And Jesus is going to make him win, because He likes a fast horse just as much as you do!"

"I'm going to put on something sexy and jump over another tractor," Clotilde mumbled.

"Oy vay!" Sam Seventeen croaked through his mask. "Get me a doctor right now! I gotta live for all this!"

***

As the night of Regimental Mint's second race approached, the roster of Reggie's Regiment diligently prepared for the event.

Lana spent every evening with Ryan O'Bryan, and fell interminably in love.

Ryan, who was already interminably in love with Lana, explained to his grandfather that he was only going to get married once. Any other females in his life were going to be horses.

Absinth dyed her hair blue, because it went better with pink.

Nettie read textbooks about equine evolution and thanked God for her newly discovered insight into reality. She bought some red cowgirl boots that matched the little ribbons in her hair.

Clotilde stopped flushing her medications down the toilet and began to study fashion magazines. She discovered very quickly that pink might look okay on Absinth, but it would clash with big green tractors. She inventoried her purse and then called a Neiman Marcus consultant for a makeover.

Ten Horse Tales

Reggie went to Papillon Assisted Living Center every morning and studied the Daily Racing Form with Sam Seventeen. They had accumulated nearly two thousand dollars in winnings between them before the day that Regimental Mint was to race, and on the day of the race they decided to put it all on Regimental Mint's nose. Such a bet might push the odds down a little, but they didn't care because they were confident of a win. Their horse's number would be five.

The evening of the race was oddly different than expected, because nobody went to the track except Lana, who had to place bets for Reggie's Regiment and then coach Regimental Mint in his race. The rest of the owning partners gathered in Sam Seventeen's room to be with their friend that was constrained by failing health from enjoying the sights, sounds, smells, and exhilarations of the racetrack.

Sam Seventeen had always dreamed of owning his own racehorse and being with fellow horsemen in the winner's circle. He was flattered and touched that his friends chose to be with him for this sure-to-be-great race instead of being at the track for certain imminent glory. The ladies of the partnership were all decked out in their Sunday best, and he nearly choked when he saw the transformation that Clotilde had made.

So did Reggie.

So did Ryan O'Bryan.

So did Absinth and Nettie.

Clotilde stepped into the misty hissing antiseptic aura of Sam Greenberg's obligate repository, and it was as though she had emerged from the cover of *Vanity Fair*. Neiman Marcus, and her resumed medical regimen, had done her proud. She carried a little green umbrella, for reasons that only Neiman Marcus knew, and she leaned on it when she bent over to speak to Sam

Seventeen. Her lipstick was a shade of yellow that complimented green.

"We are going to win a lot of money tonight, Sam Seventeen," the perfectly coifed, silver-haired, transformed lady said in unwavering soprano. "You have always been my friend here at Papillon, and so I bought you a two thousand dollar wager on Reginald Minty's nose. When you win, I'd like my principle back, because I'm going to buy some more racehorses first thing next week. Oh, does anybody here have any idea where one can buy a good racehorse?" She looked over to Reggie and melted him with a solid warm smile.

Everyone crowded around the television set that had been set up in Sam Seventeen's room. The six-length win by number five, Regimental Mint, was almost anticlimactic after the anticipative banter that had been passed around the room by his excited owners. The champagne glasses with Dr. Pepper were clinked and drained as happy horse owners tallied their winnings in their minds.

They had recorded the race on tape, and they played it over and over again. Regimental Mint won the race every time they replayed it, and they cheered every win as though it was the first. Sam Seventeen breathed one hundred per cent oxygen to keep from turning blue while he cheered for the fastest, and only, horse that he had ever owned. And the evening got even better when Lana finally arrived from the track.

Lana had insisted that no one but herself, a groom, and the jockey be in Regimental Mint's win picture. She took a picture of Sam Seventeen that Ryan had found in an old album and had the track photographer insert it into the winning picture in place of the groom. The result was a winner's circle picture with Sam Seventeen proudly holding the reins of his winning horse. She presented this picture, framed in silver, to an ecstatic Samuel Greenberg, who had once been the obscure seventeenth listing in a phonebook and was now the owner of a certified Thoroughbred winner. He was also the grandfather of the man Lana loved.

***

Sam Seventeen died during the night that was the happiest of his life, and he had pink and red and yellow lipstick on his forehead to show for it. In his final repose, he held the picture of himself and Regimental Mint in both hands.

A few weeks later Ryan and Lana O'Bryan met Reggie and Clotilde Ridgewood at the Keeneland Horse Sale, and together they paid a quarter of a million dollars for a yearling that they named Sam Seventeen.

Sam Seventeen was to become the fastest two-year-old in the barn, and Reggie Ridgewood came to realize that he was going to live forever.

WIND

Chuck was a seven year old who lived with his parents and two older sisters at the Sunny Lake Mobile Home Park. Sunny Lake was an old but fairly well kept place, with a few occupied singlewides, and several vacant lots. Tenants were supposed to maintain their own lots, but few rarely did. Chuck's father, a one-armed man who tried his best to provide for his family, mowed the vacant lots and chopped down weeds around the fences for a few dollars a day, and many times he would go ahead and mow some old lady's little yard or sweep some sick person's sidewalk out of the goodness of his heart. Chuck helped his father on weekends and summer mornings and knew all the ins and outs of the mobile home park. There was no sunny lake, nor even a pond, but in the far back of the park there was a little creek that ran along a draw just beyond the property line. Chuck's idea of a fun time was playing in that creek, but his parents had forbidden him to go there alone because of the Indian.

Mr. Ten Rattles lived in a nineteen-fifties-vintage two-wheeled recreational trailer at the very back of the mobile home park. Trees and shrubs nearly hid the little camper on the lot where nobody from Sunny Lake dared to tread. Mr. Ten Rattles kept his old mare on the enclosed grassy field between the Sunny Lake back property line and the tree line along the creek. Rumor had it that the ancient Native American took serious umbrage to anyone who dared cross his field to get to the isolated creek, and would boil and eat anyone who dared touch his precious old mare.

Chuck rarely disobeyed his parents, but on some summer days he yielded to his yearnings for the creek and sneaked around the fence line of the Ten Rattles field to the shady draw and the creek that ran through it. Whenever he did that, he noticed that the old mare would immediately come over and walk the fence line with him. When he would get to the creek, she would stand inside her fence and wait for him to return home. An ancient pear tree growing in the creek bed began to drop fruit in early August, and Chuck soon learned that the mare loved pears. He would find one for her when he got to the creek, and when he finished doing whatever little boys do when playing in the woods, he would gather several smaller pears and feed them to her over the fence one at a time as they walked back around the perimeter of the field to the trailer park.

Chuck decided that he didn't need to walk clear around the field to get to the creek, so one August morning he broke all rules of tradition and parental admonition and cut directly across the field. The mare walked beside him, and he put his hand on her shoulder as they trudged along. He kind of held her to the side so she wouldn't step on his little feet. She waited patiently at the far fence while he looked for a fresh firm pear for her. He turned several pears over and found that they had been gnawed on by wild creatures, or had spoiled after hitting the ground. Some pears were covered with ants. Finally he found an enormous yellow-green one that appeared to be perfect, and he stooped to pick it up with both hands. When he stood up, he found himself looking into the brown weather-scarred face of a true, and frowning, American Indian. He dropped his pear and stood terrified as his mother's admonitions about cannibals in the woods ripped through his mind.

"That's a nice pear, small white man," the Indian said without changing his expression. "Rain would like to eat that one."

Chuck instantly deduced that the mare's name was Rain. "I'll just take it to her then," he said as he picked it up, "if it's okay with you, Mr. Ten Rattles."

"Don't call me Ten Rattles, small man," the Indian boomed. "Not good manners. Only Chickasaw can call me by Indian name."

Chuck cringed. His parents had taught him to display good manners in the presence of adults, but he had no concept of mannerly response to someone who momentarily may very well eat him. "What should I call you, Sir?" he said timidly.

"Call me Sig," the big dark man said, and he almost smiled.

"Sig? Is that an Indian name?"

"Sig be white man's nickname for Chickasaw name, Siegfried."

"What does Siegfried mean in Indian, Sig?"

"Siegfried is Chickasaw word for 'that baby's daddy is a German.' What is your name, small white man?"

"Charles Dickens Wainwright the Fourth! I live at lot seventeen in the Sunny Lake Mobile Home Park." That much he knew from rote. To impress his new friend, he added a few facts he had learned about his family. "My daddy's great-grandfather made oxcarts! He had two hands. Everybody calls me Chuck, though."

"Okay, Chuck. Give Rain her pear. Then you help me gather some reeds from the creek bed."

Chuck held the pear through the fence for the old mare to chomp. The pear was large, and she took several bites to get it all down.

Chuck, suddenly proud of himself for befriending the dreaded Indian by catering to his horse, turned from the fence and walked back to the old man. "What are we going to do with reeds, Sig?"

"I am going to make a halter for Wind," the Indian said.

"You're going to try to catch the wind? How're you going to do that?"

"Help. Not talk. Maybe *you* will be the one to halter Wind."

Sig cut the reeds, and Chuck placed them in a pile with all the stems in one direction. Sig then showed the boy how to strip the reeds into long tough fibers. When they finished the work, Sig bound the fibers into a huge bale, dropped it over the fence, climbed over the fence and then threw it over his shoulder to carry it home. The wily Indian instructed Chuck to bring along an armload of pears to draw the mare's attention away from the bale of fibers, which looked to her like hay.

They crossed the field to the trailer park and, when they arrived, Chuck knew that he would catch unshirted hell from his parents if he went to the Indian's home. He waved goodbye to the old man and skipped down the crumbling roadway to lot seventeen.

At dinner, Chuck's mother served up some roast beef sandwiches that she had brought from the restaurant where she worked as a waitress. Chucks father loved to eat sandwiches for dinner, because they were inexpensive, and because Chuck's mother would cut them into fourths for him so he could eat them easily with his only hand.

"So what did you do this afternoon, Chuck," his mother asked as she sat down beside him to frown over her sandwich, which resembled all four hundred of the other ones she had served that day.

"I met a new friend. His name is Sig."

"Sig? That's a German name, isn't it?"

"Yes, Ma'am, it is. He told me his daddy was a German."

"So what did you and Sig do today."

"We picked reeds to make string with. We're going to make things with it."

"Really now," Chuck's father said quizzically. "And where would you be finding reeds?"

Chuck gulped. "Down by the creek."

"I thought I told you not to go down there by yourself, Chuck."

"I wasn't alone, Dad. I was with Sig."

"Okay, Honey," Chuck's mother said. "You need to bring Sig over to the house to play sometime soon."

"I don't think so, Mom. I don't think you'd like him very much."

Mom raised her eyebrows. "And why would that be?"

"He doesn't talk much, and he never smiles."

***

With the resumption of school, Chuck's weekday time became fully occupied, and he didn't get to visit with his elderly friend much. The grass stopped growing when autumn came to the trailer park, but the weeds didn't. Chuck's father went out to cut them down on October Saturday mornings. The one-armed man could wield a Weed-eater deftly, and he could even handle a rake. But Chuck had to load the piles of cut weeds into a wheelbarrow and steer it with both hands to the burn-pile that was located at the back of the property, near the Indian's overgrown lot. The weeds were never burned, though. The big piles just disappeared.

Chuck knew that the Indian had a goat in a little pen in the trees on his lot, and the old man would come over and scoop them up for his pet after dark. The goat was black, but his name was Snow. Snow was always a hardship for Plains Peoples, Sig had explained, and goats were always a pain in the rear; hence his name.

On the first Saturday of December, Chuck and his father were doing yard work around the trailer park manager's office. The office was located near the entrance to the park, in the only doublewide unit in the entire mobile park. Needa Gormly, the park manager, came out of the office and called to them.

"Charles, I need to talk to you for a minute. Come in and bring Chuck in, too."

Needa had a large desk in the office, and Chuck and his father sat down in two chairs in front of it. Chuck's father had an anxious expression on his face.

"Would you like some hot tea," Needa offered.

"No, thank you," Chuck's father said.

"No, thank you," Chuck said, aping his father.

"Sure you do; it's cold outside," Needa said as she poured some tea for each of them anyway. She was a large affable woman, and she was Charles Wainwright's boss, so the one-armed father did not protest. "Here's some sugar for you," she said.

Chuck took a spoonful of sugar and stirred it into his tea noisily, like little boys do. His father reached over and silently removed the spoon from his cup as Needa took her seat behind the big desk.

Ten Horse Tales

"So, Charles," the manager said to Chuck's father, "How are things going for you in these troubled economic times."

"Well, I don't get many hours at my part-time job at the cemetery cuz the grass don't grow when it's cold. Cindy Lou is working full time at the sandwich place, but people ain't tipping very good, she says. This here job keeps us eating, quite frankly."

Needa realized that Charles was fearful of losing his grounds-keeping job, and she smiled kindly. "That's why I called you two in here. You know who Ten Rattles is, Charles. He's old as dirt, and he's suffering from arthritis since the weather changed. He asked me to ask you if little Chuck could help him take care of his horse. He said he'd pay fifty dollars a week if Chuck would give him an hour of help every day."

"Fifty dollars!" Chuck's father whistled through his teeth. "Where'd that old Indian get that kind of money?"

"He's got it, Charles. He never spends any. He doesn't even have a television."

"Why my Chuck? There's lotsa older kids around the trailer park."

"Chuck is the only person in this park, besides me, that has ever spoken to him. He likes Chuck."

Charles' eyes narrowed into a frown. "I thought I told you to stay away from that Indian's place," he said to his son.

"That's where the weed pile is, Daddy. He asked me if he could have the weeds for his goat. He was very nice. He wouldn't hurt me." This was stretching the truth a little, but it wasn't a lie. Chuck would never lie to his father."

"The boy is right, Charles. I've known Ten Rattles since the day I started working here. He's harmless. Everyone is suspicious of him because he keeps to himself. When he was younger and less sickly, he would run out and cuss at people if they bothered his horse, and everybody was scared to death of him. Now he needs some help, and it seems to me that he'll pay handsomely for it. Surely you can use fifty more dollars a week."

"That'll buy Chuck and his sisters some clothes, and maybe we can start putting some money in the kids' savings accounts again. Yeah, okay. Chuck can help the old guy if he wants to."

"Oh boy! I'll go over there right now." The excited child jumped up, sipped his coat, and ran out the door.

Needa laughed. "Don't you worry, Charles. I know Ten Rattles well. Everything is going to be just fine."

***

The old man took Chuck to the shed behind his little trailer. Rain's house was ramshackle on the outside, but inside there were two large stalls, a stack of hay bales, a room full of sacked feed, and a place for halters, lead lines, and grooming equipment. The warm shed smelled like leather and horse manure and molasses. Chuck couldn't wait to learn how to do his chores.

Ten Rattles showed him how to measure feed and how much hay to mete out. He showed him how to clean the stall and wash out Rain's water bucket. This was much easier to do when Rain was turned out into the field. But Rain liked to roll in the mud when she was turned out, so Chuck learned how to hose her off and brush her before she came back to her stall. After he put the mare up, he would open the shed door into Ten Rattles' yard and let Snow, the goat, into the shed where it was warm. Rain and Snow were good friends, it seems, and the goat slept by the door of the mare's stall.

Chuck had earned one hundred and fifty dollars for his family by Christmas time, so their Christmas Eve dinner in their singlewide abode was a very happy one. On Christmas morning, though, it was business as usual for the little boy, because Rain had no concept of holidays. There was a light snow on the ground when he trundled over to the shed.

Ten Rattles was sitting on a stool in the aisle waiting for him. He had a pile of dried reed fibers in his lap, and he was trying to weave something with his arthritic hands."

"Merry Christmas, Sig!" the seven-year-old shouted with a smile.

"Ugh," said the old Indian. "Wind come soon. Much work to do."

"What work, Sig? What do we have to do now?"

"Take stall panel out. Make one big stall."

Ten Rattles showed Chuck how to take the screws out of the boards that separated the two stalls in the shed. The old man's fingers were gnarled and painful, and he simply could not grasp the screwdriver firmly enough to turn the screw heads.

Chuck was just a little kid, so he had to use both hands to get a screw to come loose. The old man balanced the board so it wouldn't fall on the boy before all the screws were out. This was a painfully slow process, and they only got two boards down. There were fourteen big slabs of treated lumber left.

"Must have boards out by January fifteen, boy. Wind come."

"My hands hurt too much now to take out another screw," Chuck confessed. "I'll try to get some of them out for you every day, Sig. I still don't understand about what the wind has to do with this."

"Come, boy. Time for lesson." Ten Rattles put his hand on the boy's shoulder and led him out of the shed and across a snowy path to his little trailer.

Chuck had never been in the little one-room camper. There was a small bed, a chair, a sink with a counter that served as a table, and a door that apparently went into a tiny bathroom. There was also a file cabinet with some books stacked on it.

Ten Rattles picked up a huge magnifying glass and studied the titles on his books. He chose one ancient book with a time-bleached and unraveling cover. He carefully turned the brown pages until he found what he was looking for. He handed the open book to Chuck and said, "Read."

"I'm only seven, Sig. I don't *read* very well."

"No problem, Chuck. Indian who write book not *write* very well."

The title of the book was *SPIRITS*. The page Chuck was to read was titled *WIND*. Chuck read hesitatingly as he made out the words.

"Wind is clean and good. Wind makes music in the treetops, carries birds to the sky, draws pictures in the snow, and makes waves on the lakes. In winter, Wind carries the cold with anger; rain turns to sleet and ice, trees bend, and man and beast cower to a roar louder than thunder. In spring, Wind carries warmth to the land as He runs through the greening fields in playful circles and dashes across the plains with gusts of joy. Neither birds nor horses can run faster than a determined Wind."

"What does de-ter-mined mean, Sig?"

"It means setting your mind to a task and then getting it done. Like, we have to finish taking down those boards before January fifteenth, and it will get done. Or like this! I started weaving these reeds in the summer. I was determined to finish in time for Wind, and I did it!" The old Indian had never spoken to Chuck so eloquently before. He held up a tiny firmly-woven halter and grinned broadly."

The light dawned for Chuck. "Wind is a baby horse? That's it! Wind will be determined to run like a Wind Spirit, faster than all the other horses!"

Ten Rattles pursed his lips and furrowed his brow in mock perplexity. "Small white man getting smart," he said dourly.

***

The old Indian and the little boy removed the last screw from the last board in the stall partition on the evening of Friday, January twelfth. The stall was now doubled in size, and the crippled old man and the seven-year-old boy had prepared for the coming of Wind without anyone else's help. They put an extra thick covering of straw on the stall floor."

"Now we wait," the Indian said with his usual inscrutable expression. "I stay night, you stay day. Maybe one of us see Wind come." The mare watch had begun.

Chuck hurried through his breakfast on Saturday morning and ran through the slushy snow to Ten Rattles' barn with unabated anticipation.

The old man was sitting on his stool weaving a halter one size bigger than the one he had already made. He had his feet propped on the goat's back. "No Wind today," he said gruffly. "Rain making milk now. Maybe Wind come tomorrow."

Chuck couldn't hide his disappointment, but he grabbed a muck rack and began to clean Rain's stall.

After paying Chuck for the previous week's work, Ten Rattles went home to get some rest after staying up with the mare all night with no reward of a newborn.

Chuck went home for lunch with his family. He found everyone in a somber mood, because his gardener father wasn't getting any working hours when there was snow on the ground. He gave his brand new fifty dollar bill to his mother, who seemed to brighten up a little as she stuffed it into a cookie jar in the cupboard. "Why do babies take so long to come?" he asked.

"God just does it that way," his mother said. "That baby horse will get here when God is ready."

"Sometimes God does things in funny ways," the child said as he glanced over at his one-armed father, who was struggling to spread jam on his toast.

Charles Dickens Wainwright the Third looked his son in the eye sternly. "That Indian isn't teaching you heathen ideas about God, is he?"

"No Daddy. All he talks about is the wind."

Chuck went back to the barn and stayed until dark. Rain ate a lot of feed and hay, but otherwise spent the afternoon snoozing. Ten Rattles came to the barn in time for Chuck to go home for dinner.

"Weather changing," the old Indian said. "Gonna get real cold. Maybe Wind come tonight."

Chuck went home, ate dinner and went straight to bed.

It was still dark outside when he awoke on Sunday morning. The wind was rattling the roof of the mobile home, and the floor was ice cold when Chuck's bare feet found it. The anxious little boy put on his heaviest clothes and warmest coat and sneaked out of the house before his parents awakened. He trudged through two inches of new snow to get to the horse shed.

Inside the shed, he saw Rain standing quietly in her stall, and Ten Rattles was asleep on the aisle floor with his head on Snow the goat's belly. He walked to the stall and peeked inside. A chestnut foal with four white socks was nursing on the mare.

Chuck's heart pounded with excitement. He shook the old Indian and the goat at the same time, and they both tried to scramble to their feet. Snow bounded up quickly, but Ten

Ten Horse Tales

Rattles, still half asleep, had to be assisted to an upright stance by Chuck.

"Look, Sig! Wind is here. When did he come, Sig?"

Ten Rattles wiped his eyes and peered into the stall. He shook his head to get the sleep out when he saw the foal. He waited several seconds before answering, but then turned to Chuck and nodded his head gravely in approval. "Not know when come, but she is here. I have to go call a vet."

Wind was a filly, and appeared robust and healthy. Chuck ran back to the house to get his parents and sisters to come to see her. Before they got to the barn, the veterinarian had already showed up to check the mare and her newborn foal. Everyone marveled at the perfection of the filly, but Ten Rattles stayed true to his reclusion and did not return to the barn while anyone else was there.

The morning of Wind's birth, January fourteenth, was also the time of the last winter storm of the new year. The sun came out, the snow melted, and the Wind Spirits dried out the mud so Rain and her baby could romp in the field within four days of the birth event. Chuck and Ten Rattles stood in the sunshine by the fence and watched the frisky foal run circles around her mother as they played in the new winter grass.

"Wind good name for filly, Small Chuck. Jockey Club thinks so, too. This Wind is fast. Remember book? Nothing runs faster than Wind."

Chuck had never been to a horserace in his life, but he knew in his heart that Ten Rattles was right. Ten Rattles had doubled Chuck's salary when the horse population in back of Sunny Lake Mobile Home Park doubled, so the boy spent every waking hour that he wasn't in school fussing over the mare and foal and listening to Ten Rattles' pronouncements about horsemanship.

He thought it was amazing that just as Ten Rattles finished weaving a new halter, Wind had grown large enough for it to fit. Chuck turned eight in March, and he had already determined that he was going to be a horseman when he grew up.

Warmth came with spring breezes, but for unexplainable reasons, spring also brought failure to Ten Rattles' health. Ten Rattles swore Chuck to secrecy about his illness, because he did not want anybody to insinuate themselves into his reclusive life. One evening in April, Chuck realized that he had not seen his elderly friend all day, so he went to Ten Rattles' little trailer to check on him.

He found the old man lying quietly on his bed with the *SPIRITS* book on his chest. He could barely speak, but when he did, Chuck was very surprised at his diction.

"I can't see to read my book, Chuck," he said weakly. "Would you please read to me the chapter about *WIND*? I want to go to sleep with Wind at my back."

Chuck took the book and read the chapter aloud. He glanced over and saw that Ten Rattles was smiling as he read. He closed the book when he finished and handed it back to the old man. "I'll read another chapter to you if you like, Sig."

"You don't have to call me Sig anymore, Charles Dickens Wainwright the Fourth," the old man said as he patted the boy on the arm. "You are as good an Indian as I am, and you are my friend, so call me Ten Rattles."

The boy leaned over and hugged his friend. "Yes Sir, Ten Rattles," he said as he choked back tears. "You're not going to leave me and Wind and Rain are you? And Snow?"

"I'll never leave any of you, Chuck. Now run down to the office and get Needa for me, and then go home like a good little Indian and go to bed."

Ten Horse Tales

"Okay, bye, Ten Rattles," he said reluctantly. He did exactly as he was told.

The following morning when Chuck went to the barn to feed the animals, his father and mother insisted on coming with him. He realized why when he saw the big black cars on the gravel roadway by the little trailer house. Chuck began to cry, so his father dished the feed rations and served the hay according to the boy's tearful instructions.

Needa came into the barn with two well-dressed men, whom she introduced to Chuck's parents as lawyers for Ten Rattles' estate. One of the men was tall and dark, and Chuck knew that he was a Native American.

"I have a letter for the Wainwright family," the dark man said somberly. "It was attached to the thirty-second codicil of his will. Mr. Ten Rattles was an important functionary of the Chickasaw Nation, and it is my duty to read this letter to you and guarantee that Mr. Ten Rattles' wishes are carried out to the letter. May I read it now?"

"Please do, Sir," Charles Wainwright said with his mouth agape in amazement.

"Before I begin, let me inform you that Mr. Ten Rattles was the owner of this Mobile Home Park and all of the property surrounding it to the extent of seven hundred acres. In other codicils of his will, he bequeaths all of the property within the trailer park to his faithful employee, Needa Gormly, and forgives the mortgage on lot seventeen for the Wainwright family. In the thirty-second codicil he is specific about large sums of money, hence this letter. Before I start reading, bear in mind that Mr. Ten Rattles was the recipient of enormous oil royalties from holdings within the Chickasaw Nation, and his reclusive style of living belied the vastness of his wealth. He wanted to be alone in his waning years, but apparently young Charles became a friend that he cherished. The letter states as follows:

"By way of explanation, this letter concerns the thirty-second codicil which I have placed into my last will and testament because my dear friend, Charles Dickens Wainwright the Fourth, deserves some support in order to carry out my wishes. The codicil remands to the care of his guardians the property that I own behind the trailer park, the barn thereon, the Registered Thoroughbred mare named Rain, and the Registered Thoroughbred filly named Wind. I have also allocated the sum of two hundred thousand dollars to be used to support these horses so long as they shall live, and another two hundred thousand dollars to be remanded to Charles Dickens Wainwright the Fourth on the day of his legal majority, to be used as he deems fit. I will be with Wind, in the wind behind her backside, when she runs. The Spirits are with you, Chuck, so your good fortune, too, rides on the Spring Wind; warm, eternal, and determined! Thanks for your friendship toward this old Indian. Siegfried Ten Rattles"

THE ONE THAT GOT AWAY

Trinidad Reilly and Ashwood Forrest had become fast friends when they were little boys working for their fathers on the backside of Texas racetracks. They mucked stalls together, groomed horses together, and went to school on the bus together. When they weren't working or studying, they went fishing together. Friends and family knew them as Trini and Tree.

Both men had married swing-shift nurses, so after work every day they met at the simulcast parlor to eat dinner and then watch and handicap the horse races until their wives got home at midnight. They always made enough money betting on the ponies to pay for boat rental for weekend fishing forays. The objective of their betting was always to make enough money to rent a large enough boat that their wives would feel comfortable in coming along if they had the weekend off.

At the simulcast parlor, Trini and Tree hung out in the non-smoking section with Arnie Monkford, who was wheelchair bound because of chronic heart and lung problems. Arnie was the best handicapper at the parlor. He set a goal of four hundred dollars in profit every night, and he quit betting when he reached it. Rare was the occasion when he had to place bets on the last race of the evening. Arnie shared his factual knowledge generously with his friends, but he never revealed exactly which horse he was going to bet on, or in what order he had placed his exacta and trifecta choices.

One Friday evening all three of the friends were having an unusually unproductive run of luck.

"Looks like we'll be renting a rowboat tomorrow," Trini said dejectedly.

"You'll have to come along and paddle for us," Tree said to Arnie with a grin.

Arnie had never gone fishing with them before and, because of his medical paraphernalia, he likely never would. "My oxygen tanks would sink a little rowboat, and I would go down like a crab trap," the dyspneic invalid replied with a shudder. "You'd have to rent a trawler the size of the Queen Mary before I'd ever get on it. Maybe you ought to try for a superfecta win tonight, Trini. That would make up for your losses and pay for a fine skiff tomorrow."

"I haven't even been able to pick *two* horses tonight," Trini lamented. "I seriously doubt that the gods would bless me with *four* in tandem! Nah, I think Lady Luck ain't with me tonight, Arnie. You got any special god connections?"

Arnie laughed. "I've already prayed to God, Allah, Zeus, Hera and Mars, and the ponies aren't hearing their exhortations. Buddha and Ahuramazda didn't answer my prayers, either. I guess we could try Wodan or Poseidon."

Tree grimaced. "If my memory serves me correctly, Wodan was married to someone named Frigg. I think we've had enough of that already tonight!"

Trini appreciated Tree's cleverness, so he allowed himself to laugh in spite of the dour run of luck that was about to send him home with less money than he came with. "So that leaves

Poseidon. I thought Poseidon was an upside-down boat in some movie. What could he do for us tonight?"

"Poseidon is the Ocean God of Greek mythology," Arnie explained as he downed a huge gulp of draught beer. "The Romans called him Neptune. Maybe ole Poseidon would want you to come fishing in his backyard in an upscale boat tomorrow. Ask him to find a good race for you to bet on and guide you to the four horses that are going to light the board."

Tree jumped up excitedly and started rummaging through his various race programs. "Hey, I just remembered that Poseidon was also the god of horses. And I saw something on one of these cards a while ago...yeah, here it is. It's the tenth race at Dallas. A maiden claimer with twelve horses and two of them are ninety-to-one long shots! One long shot is named Ocean Potion and the other is named Foamy Wave. Both are by obscure sires out of unraced mares nobody ever heard of. They're in pole positions eleven and twelve, which is as bad as it gets for starting positions."

Trini brightened up as he perused the data about the pending race. He had seen the favorite fade in the stretch on several occasions, and the second favorite hadn't raced for five months, which meant to him that the colt was coming off an injury and might not be in top form. "I think you've got something here, Tree. Let's buy four ten-dollar tickets pairing the long shots to win, with the favorites to run third and fourth. Nobody else in the whole world would make those bets, so if we win we'll get the whole pool!"

Arnie frowned and shook his head. "Nobody else is going to make that bet because everybody else in the whole world knows it can't happen. That's forty bucks down the drain, y'all. You're not handicapping now; you're playing hunches based on mythology! I mean, this praying to Poseidon thing is stretching it a little, don't you think."

Tree assumed a pensive poise. "We talk about a god of the seas that was also once revered as the protector of horses. Then along comes a race with horses with ninety-to-one odds and mariner names! Jeez, Arnie, it's an omen! You gotta place a bet here!"

"I'm for it," Trini said as he fished in his pocket for twenty dollars. "Give me another twenty, Tree, and I'll bet it for the two of us if Arnie doesn't want to play. Hell, we ain't gonna have to declare bankruptcy if we lose forty bucks. It's Friday, so our wives will be bringing home paychecks tonight anyway. Let's see if we can top their week's pay with a seahorse hit!"

Arnie shrugged his shoulders and took a long breath out of his oxygen mask. "If you're going to make a stupid bet, just put two dollars on the long shot's noses. Betting them both to top off a superfecta is insanity."

"Sane handicapping hasn't paid off tonight," Trini said through a silly grin. "Maybe a stupid hunch will be a good thing. I'm going to go place my bets."

"Wait a minute, Trini," Arnie called. "Here's four bucks. Put two bucks each for me on eleven and twelve to place." Arnie's grin was sheepish as he handed Trini the bills. "Well, my bet isn't quite as stupid as yours," he said as he turned his wheelchair toward the video screen that was displaying the Dallas meet.

The eleven and twelve horses came out of the gate ahead of the others and moved to the rail to set the pace around the first turn. The two favorites fell in behind them and remained just off the pace down the backstretch. All four horses picked up speed around the second turn and left the remaining eight in the dust as they headed down the stretch to the wire. Turn of foot notwithstanding, the favorites could not catch the long shots, and number eleven, Ocean Potion, edged out number twelve, Foamy Wave, by a neck!

Arnie had turned blue as he held his breath during the stretch run. He gulped at his oxygen between whoops of joy as he realized that he had won nearly a hundred dollars on a four-dollar place bet.

Trini's and Tree's joy was unrestrained when the two long shots crossed the wire ahead of the two favorites to complete a superfecta that every handicapper dreams of. The payoff was thirty-two thousand dollars.

Everybody in the simulcast parlor rushed over to congratulate the winners, and Trini began to buy a round of beers for all of his less lucky friends and celebrants.

"I can't believe it!" Arnie gurgled as he tried to keep his mask on while Trini and Tree hugged him. "You are the luckiest S.O.B.s in Christendom."

"Ole Poseidon came through for us, by golly," Tree shouted over the din. "I'm going to rent the biggest boat in Galveston tomorrow so you can come along, Arnie."

Arnie crossed himself. "No, thanks, Tree. I'm going to come here tomorrow and handicap horses like I always do. I've had enough of Poseidon already."

***

Trini's and Tree's wives both drew Saturday shifts, so the men had to go fishing by themselves. They had given their delighted wives half their winnings, and still had plenty of money to rent a forty-foot sedan fishing boat for the weekend. By noon Trini was in the pilot's seat heading out into the Gulf of Mexico where he knew the big fish hung out. Tree prepared the tackle and began to dream of the big one that he was going to haul in.

Their luck was at its fulminating best and the sun was shining, so this had to be a banner day for fishing in the blue-green sea.

But the joy of the superfecta win began to fade as the day dwindled into twilight and no denizen of the gulf expressed interest in snapping at bait offerings of two tiring fishermen. The sound of lapping waves and the smell of diesel fumes began to lull them into somnolence, and Trini decided to stop the boat and shut down the engines while they took a break from trolling.

"Seems like old Poseidon isn't interested in our company today, Tree. I've never gone a whole afternoon without even a bite. This beautiful boat is going to waste!"

Tree propped his huge rod and reel between his knees and relaxed back into his ergonomically designed fighting chair. "Why don't you go to the galley, Trini, and fix us some sandwiches. Lets drink a couple of beers and try our luck just sitting here with the bait hanging deep in the water."

Trini fixed some hot dogs and snacks and brought them out to the deck along with his Daily Racing Form. "Maybe we ought to go on in before it gets dark. We could get down a couple of bets before the girls get home from work. We still have enough money to rent this boat another time."

"Yeah, you're probably right," Tree answered. "I'll say a little prayer to Poseidon while I eat my sandwich. If we don't get a nibble in the next twenty minutes we can go back and get some excitement with the ponies. Maybe that's where the mossy old goat's heart is today."

Suddenly Tree's fishing rod flexed downward, and the reel, which was between his knees, began to feed out line with a squealing whine. Tree jumped to grab the handle of the rod, and his bun, wiener and relish went twirling through the air over the transom into the water. He caught the rod by the grips in front of the reel, wrestled its lower handle into the gimbal in the footrest of his fighting chair, and planted his feet firmly on the sturdy foot-rest to support his body for the pending contest.

"Whoa, you got something big on there!" Trini shouted. "He's pulling the boat backwards! Should I start the engines?"

"No, don't do that, Trini. He might foul the line in the props. Let me pull on him a little and see if we can get him to surface!"

At that moment a dark squall rolled over the water toward the boat, and the wind tossed salty spray as lightning struck the ocean surface with a thunderous blast not far from their location. Clouds blocked out the sunlight, and a cold rain began to pelt the excited fishermen. Tree's knuckles turned white as he tugged on his lurching rod.

Trini yelled at his partner. "Keep that pole anchored in the gimbal and get him surfaced quick, Tree! We're going to have to deal with him and a storm at the same time. I've got to start the engines soon to keep control of the boat!"

Tree's arms had already started to ache as he tugged on the rod. "This be a big bugger, Trini! He's gonna surface when he wants to!"

Trini buckled Tree into his chair so he wouldn't get pulled over the transom as the boat pitched in the waves. "Ole Poseidon's gonna make it tough for us, Tree!" he shouted over another thunderclap. "I'm gonna start the engines and navigate these waves while you work!" Trini skittered across the deck and disappeared into the sanctuary of the pilothouse to go about getting some power.

Foamy waves splashed over the deck, and the rain was suddenly freezing into hail when Tree's prey finally became visible on the water's surface. A flat whale-like tail that was almost as wide as the boat's stern extended out of the waves and crashed down with incredible force in an effort to propel its owner back into the depths. Trini was looking back over his shoulder when he saw the tail emerge, and he accelerated the boat forward slightly to try to aid Tree in pulling the catch to the surface. This pull against the denizen of the deep nearly separated Tree's arms from their sockets, but the scrappy fisherman held on with both hands and suddenly the whole creature rose up out of the sea. Tree, partially blinded by the salt water whipping across his eyes, frantically reeled in the line that had suddenly gone slack, and for a moment he thought his catch had gotten away. But Trini could see clearly, and his knees nearly buckled when he saw the head of Tree's sea monster rise above the transom. Tree gave a last tug as he wiped the salt out of his eyes with his sleeve and found himself staring into the face of a giant, and very unhappy, horse!

The animal's head was wider than Tree's chair, and seaweed dangled from its ears and mane. Its eyes were burning red, and though it was six feet away, Tree could feel its hot breath through the buffeting wind; a breath that smelled like fish-infused kerosene as it was exhaled forcefully into the face of the stunned captor.

"Holy...Trini! Trini! Help me, Trini!" Tree screamed just as the creature hoisted two hoofed legs over the side of the boat and hung there glaring at him. The stern of the boat dipped dangerously near the surface of the ocean as the monster's weight settled on the transom.

Lightning struck nearby as Trini ran out to the stern deck and grabbed the back of Tree's chair for support while the wind blew and the boat lurched. His eyes bugged when he got a close look at the sea horse. It was black with wet shiny fur. Its hooves were shod with glittering gold, and it was wearing a bridle of woven seaweed with golden buckles. The large fishhook had snagged the bridle through one of the ring-like buckles and the creature had been unable to shake it off. The seaweed reins were neatly draped over its neck, and Trini was enormously relieved to see that no one was astride its mossy back.

"He's gonna swamp the boat!" Tree shouted. Cut the line!"

The creature continued to eye them both, but didn't make any effort to pull the hind end of its body over the transom. Its whale-like tail undulated on the surface and supported most of its weight, which kept the stern of the boat from going beneath the water.

"That fishhook is close to his eye," Trini shouted. Trini was a horseman first and foremost, and he noticed things like that. "If we cut the line, that hook will irritate the hell out of him, and it might even damage his eye. Let me get it out of the bridle."

Tree leaned back as far as the chair would let him and cringed as the creature continued to breathe into his face through the rain and semi-darkness. "Are you daft, Trini? He's gonna kill us or drown us while you're farting around. Jeez!"

The animal bared his teeth when Trini put his hand out to it.

"Whoa! Whoa, Big Guy! We're sorry we caught you! Hold still and I'll get the hook out." Trini kept his hand where the creature could see it as he slowly approached the sea horse's head. The boat continued to pitch and roll, and Trini steadied himself with one hand on Tree's chair arm as he reached up to the creature and prayed that his hand wouldn't be bitten off. "Hey, your daddy Poseidon wants me to get this hook out, okay? Steady, boy. Steady there."

Amazingly, the creature's eyes softened, and it lowered its nose so Trini's hand could reach the hook. At the same moment, the wind and rain stopped, and a sunburst suddenly lit up the sea. Trini reached out and grasped the hook by its shank and guided it backward out of the buckle. The creature was free, but it did not move.

Tree breathed a sigh of relief, but he still didn't try to get out of his chair. "Well, what do we do now, Trini? There's no way we can push him back over the stern, and we can't rev the engines or he'll get cut in the propellers. My God, Trini, can you believe this! If we live through it, who's going to believe it?"

"I don't care what anyone believes," Trini said soberly. "This whole weekend has been so weird that even I may not want to believe it. But I'm believing it at this moment, because a *merhorse*, or whatever you call it, is hanging on the side of my boat and I don't know how to get him off, and if whoever put those shoes on him shows up we're gonna be in deep doodoo."

Tree cringed at that thought. "Maybe we can feed him something and he'll go away. Got any carrots?"

"Carrots! Jeez, Tree! When's the last time you brought carrots on a fishing trip?"

"Well, what's in the galley? Go look in the fridge, Trini. And hurry back before he tries to eat *me!*"

Trini scrambled back into the salon, opened the refrigerator, and took out the lunch sack that his wife had prepared for him. He dug past the wieners and buns and was amazed to discover two large red apples in the bottom of the sack. He ran out onto the deck waving them in the air.

"You're the luckiest horse in the sea," he shouted as he walked up to the now-docile creature. "See how you like this, Big Fella!" Trini rolled an apple into the creature's open jaws.

The sea monster's head was five times larger than the biggest Clydesdale head that Trini had ever seen, and the large apple fit into its mouth with room to spare. Trini jerked his hand back quickly to avoid being bitten. The big jaws crunched the apple with a resounding squish and swallowed it with a single gulp. The mer-horse nodded its head approvingly and eyed the other apple.

Trini waved it in front of the horse's flaring nostrils and stepped over to the side of the boat. The creature's eyes followed the morsel as Trini dropped it into the ocean. The incredible catch-of-the-day then smoothly withdrew its golden-shod hooves back over the stern and dived for the sinking red treat. The sea-god's mount disappeared into the deep with a thrust of its giant tail, and Trini and Tree never saw it again.

***

It was nearly ten o'clock when the two weary men wandered into the simulcast parlor. Their clothes were wrinkled and not yet dry, and they reeked of the smell of sea salt. Both wore sheepish smiles.

"Hey, look who's here," Arnie yelled from his wheelchair. "Poseidon's favorites are back from the sea. Hey, Y'all, what did you catch today."

"Nothin'," Trini said, staring at his feet. "We thought we'd come over here and try are luck with the ponies."

"Nothing? With the kind of luck you had yesterday, I thought old Poseidon would have led you to a record catch!"

"Well, I did hook one big one," Tree said with a smirk, "but it got away."

"Yeah, right," Arnie laughed, "and I'll bet Trini corroborates your story!"

"Actually, he did hook a big one, but it got unhooked," Trini said, nodding. "So, got any tips for the last races tonight, Arnie?"

"Well, I don't know, Trini. If you're still betting those crazy sea-god hunches, there's one running at Los Alamitos in about five minutes named Sea Arion Run."

Tree suddenly looked stunned. "Ye gods, Trini! Poseidon once turned himself into a horse and sired a colt named Arion!"

Both men ran toward the pari-mutuel windows as fast as they could go with their hands in their wet pockets fishing for their money clips.

THE HIGHWAYMAN

Sunday, May 8, 1774

The black-caped horseman sat astride his strangely spotted stallion and waited for the approaching coach to take visible shape in the darkness. He adjusted his black kerchief to fit high on his nose, and pulled his black hat down onto his forehead so that he could just see under the brim. On this moonless night the horse and rider were invisible beneath the trees alongside the rut-streaked Frederick Turnpike. The site was well chosen, because the coachman reined his two horses to a slow walk so as not to jostle his passengers when the carriage passed over the rough section of road. The carriage bounced and shook anyway, and the coachman was nearly unseated as be pulled on the reins with both hands to bring it to a stop. Suddenly the highwayman was directly in front of the horse team and pointing a pistol at the coachman's chest.

The driver had the barrel of a musket lying across his lap, but he could not control his reins and reach for the weapon at the same time.

"Sit still and listen well, Matey!" the rider challenged as he moved his horse alongside the carriage. "Take yer musket by its barrel and hand it down to me butt first."

The coachman obeyed, and the highwayman deftly inserted the gun into an open canvass bag attached to his saddle.

"That's a good Mate," the robber said. "Now, who ye got in the cab?"

"An English businessman who's in a hurry to get to Carrollton," the driver answered. "I told him this night travel wasn't a good idea, but he wants to be negotiating wheat contracts first thing Monday morning."

"Is he armed?"

"No, Jack. That was my job, but your bumpy road confounded my intentions."

"Lucky for you, Mate," the highwayman remarked as he began to hammer on the top of the carriage with the handle of his pistol. "Come out of the coach!" he demanded in a booming voice.

The door opened, and a frightened pudgy gentleman stepped out onto the rutty road and squinted to see into the eyes of his tormentor. "You may have my purse, Sir," he said. His hand trembled as he offered up a small leather bag for the robber to take. "I trust that you will not harm my person."

"Black Jack never harms cooperative persons; well, not on the Sabbath, anyway," the highwayman said with a laugh. "Spotty Joe and I thank ye for yer civility. Now get back in yer coach and be on yer way. And next time, be alistenin' to yer driver, Guvner. These here roads ain't safe at night."

"They're gonna be hanging ye, Black Jack," the driver said over his shoulder as he urged his horse team to forward movement.

"Don't make book on that, Matey," the highwayman shouted after him as he turned his spotted steed in the opposite direction, toward Baltimore.

A couple of miles down the Frederick Turnpike the highwayman guided his horse onto a side road that had been long abandoned. The roadway was now a weed-covered path that led to a fallow tobacco farm. The rider steered his mount to a derelict drying shed that sat decomposing near a muddy pond at the far end of the field. He dismounted, removed his cape, kerchief, and hat and stuffed them into the canvas bag before removing the saddle from his horse. He retrieved a brush from the bag and then led his horse into the shallow pond.

The horseman was a clean-shaven reddish blond man, six feet tall, in his early thirties. He wore a gray long-sleeved pullover chemise that buttoned at the collar. His riding boots extended to his knees and were apparently water proof; he was careful to step into the water no deeper than about half way up the boot tops. The spotted horse was easy to see in the opaque night, or at least he was until Black Jack the Highwayman began to scrub off the white markings.

"Be still, Joe," he said quietly as he worked the wet brush. "Our charade is almost over. Jonathon Townsend and Joe Longshanks will be leaving Black Jack and Spotty Joe here until the next waning moon. We acquired another fine musket tonight, and a pretty heavy purse, too. We're about ready to quit this business and start training for the races."

The horseman re-saddled his now dark-brown Thoroughbred, hid the canvas bag beneath a pile of rusty implements in the dilapidated barn, and rode back up the overgrown road to the turnpike. He turned right to the southeast, and headed for Baltimore at a brisk canter.

***

Monday, June 6, 1774

The new moon had not yet begun to form on this early summer night, and Black Jack had to squint into the darkness to begin the transformation of Joe Longshanks to Spotty Joe. "Let's put the white ring around your left eye tonight, Joe. It's fun to have our witnesses confound the constable. Yeah, that looks eerie enough. How about a big spot on your butt, too? Something for them to shoot at while we're running away."

Joe gave a soft nicker in response.

"Just kidding, Joe. It'll be just a minute for all this whitewash to dry and we can be on our way. Let me practice villain's jargon while we're waiting. How about 'Stand and deliver, Matey, before I blow a ball through yer gizzard!' Or maybe 'Git yer hands up if ye hanker to keep alivin!'"

Joe was not impressed and didn't bother to answer. Jack saddled him and headed for the turnpike, where he turned left toward Ellicott's Town.

Black Jack the Highwayman knew every stretch of the Frederick Turnpike like the back of his hand, and he rode to a particularly isolated dark place that he had in mind. The road here was very narrow because of tree encroachment, and it was very muddy because of a recent spring rain. Jack dismounted and tethered Spotty Joe in the darkness before crossing the road with an armful of rope. He anchored the rope to a tree head-high and then laid it across the road in the mud. He then looped the rope through the crotch of a vee-shaped oak and got a good grip on it with his gloved hands. Man and horse then waited patiently for a victim to arrive.

A farmer with a wagonload of lime from the kilns to the west sloshed by, unaware of the predators in the darkness an elbow's length away. He was allowed to pass unmolested and oblivious to his peril.

The highwayman reset his grip when he heard the sound of two trotting horses coming from the west. The riders were a red-coated British officer and his sergeant. They spurred their horses when they encountered the mud, because there was a natural inclination to get through a narrow and dark place quickly. The suddenly lifted rope raked both men off their horses and into the mud with a resounding slushy double thump.

"Whut the hell was that?" the sergeant grunted as be pulled himself to his hands and knees and wiped muck from his face with his forearm. His musket was still strapped to his back. "Are you alright, Major?"

The officer sat up in the mud and felt for his left wrist. "Damn! I think I've broken my arm, Sergeant. What has happened to us?" He was still disoriented from the fall and could discern nothing in the surrounding darkness.

"Ye're invited to meet Black Jack and Spotty Joe," a clear loud voice stated less than three feet from the officer's ear. "And ye stay where ye are, Sergeant, or I'll blow yer Major's liver out all over the road."

"You'll hang for assaulting an officer of the King, you calumnious blackguard!" the English officer shouted as he turned to look his assailant in the eyes. All he could see was a black kerchief, the low brim of a black hat, and the dangerous end of a cocked pistol.

The highwayman sniggered. "Big talk for a wounded mudpuppy, I'd say. But if they ever do hang me, Guvner, ye'll be far back in the line of them what gits to pull the trap!" Black Jack stepped over to the sergeant and pointed the pistol at his head. "Unloosen that musket belt, Sarge, and hand it to me real careful. Ye be a lucky man that yer musket didn't go off when ye fell, Sarge; it woulda blowed yer haid right off!"

"I'll be back with a brigade looking for you tomorrow, Jack; mark my words," the sergeant said defiantly as Jack took possession of his weapon.

Jack laughed heartily. "Bring lots more muskets, if ye please, Sarge. I could use some artillery, too."

"You are doing the rebellious Colonials a disservice, Sir" the major stated officiously, "by encouraging them with weaponry. King George will be hanging each and every traitor caught with a weapon, and their families, too, if this revolution actually transpires."

The highwayman stood up stiffly. "That heinous attitude, Sir, is precisely why it *will* transpire, and precisely why you *will* be ejected from the colonies." He regretted the articulate outburst before he had finished saying it, because he didn't want to give cause for the British to start looking for him amongst the educated classes. He quickly grabbed the reins of the major's horse, which had come back to where it had been stripped of its rider. He extracted a portfolio from the saddlebags, and also fished out a couple of pistols. "Hand me yer wallet wit yer good hand, Guvner, and I'll have ye on yer way."

The mud-spattered redcoat handed him his wallet, and the horseman stripped it of some pound notes.

Black Jack jeered as he handed back the empty wallet. "Since King George won't let the colonies issue paper money, ye won't mind if I use some of yers, do ye?" He turned to the sergeant, who was still on his hands and knees. "Now ye can get yer arse outta the mud and help yer gentleman onto his horse. Take him to yer company surgeon afore ye go to callin out yer artillery!"

The sergeant gave the injured major a leg up and then climbed back onto his own horse. Both soldiers then trotted off down the turnpike toward Baltimore.

"I'm truly sorry about yer arm, Guvner," Black Jack called after them, "but I'm glad ole Sarge still has his haid!"

"I'll be hanging you tomorrow, Jack," the sergeant called back. "Enjoy your own head while you still have it!"

Jack shrugged, retrieved his rope, and rode off down the pike in the same direction as the British soldiers, only not so fast. When he got to his obscure farm road, he went back to the shed, tucked away his newly obtained weapons, and washed the white spots off of Joe Longshanks' face, chest and rump. Then, dressed in common storekeeper's clothes, he pointed Joe toward Baltimore. He rode past the British barracks and saw little commotion there. *Perhaps they've had enough of Black Jack the Highwayman*, he mused. He rode through Baltimore Town to the road to Annapolis and found his place of business and home. There was a large sign on the white board-and-batten two-storied structure that invited customers into *TOWNS END SHOPPE*. He took Joe Longshanks to the carriage house behind the building, fed him a well deserved meal, and put him up for the night beside his other two horses.

***

Thursday, June 23, 1774

The tingling of his doorbell indicated to Jonathon Townsend that a customer had entered his place of business. He tucked the papers he'd been reading from the English officer's portfolio into a drawer and walked into the display room of Towns End Shoppe to greet the new arrival.

"Ah, good morning, Herr von Stueffel! How did you do at the Annapolis races?"

"I won my race, Mr. Townsend! By golly, we left them in the dust!" The tall elderly German spoke with a heavy accent. He was very well dressed, and he removed his hat as he joyfully announced his win.

"Congratulations, Herr von Stueffel! I hope you made a bold wager."

"Indeed I did, jah! Oh, Mr. Townsend, I won a lot of money! So I want to buy a gift for my wife. I always leave her at home when I go to the races, and a little present will keep me in good stead, jah?"

Von Stueffel was well known in Baltimore and Annapolis. He had immigrated with a large German contingent that settled around Frederick Township in western Maryland. He had accumulated a sizeable expanse of farm acreage, and then had discovered that his land was rich in iron ore. There was no place in Germany called Stueffel, but he had added the *von* to his name because it sounded more prestigious. One could do such a thing in the colonies and get away with it.

"I have some beautiful wine glasses from Belgium, Herr von Stueffel," Jonathon Townsend suggested. "Do you think she'd like them for her formal dinner table?"

"She has enough stems to entertain the entire Hessian Army, Mr. Townsend. I was thinking more of silver. I can pay with Pounds Sterling, and get sterling back in return. If revolution brings war and inflation, I can always melt the silverware and use it for tender."

Townsend pointed to a display case. "I have a sterling table setting for ten places that has just arrived from Boston. Designed and crafted by Mr. Revere himself, it would be a handsome compliment to Frau von Stueffel's dining parlor."

The German nodded approvingly. "I'll take that, jah. What is the price?"

"Twelve Pounds Sterling, Herr von Stueffel. You won't find better-crafted merchandise for that price anywhere in the colonies."

Von Stueffel whistled through his teeth as he reached for his heavy purse and counted out the huge sum.

Townsend smiled and winked. "Like you said, Herr von Stueffel; you can always melt forks and spoons and mint your own coins. So, when do you think the revolution is going to start?"

The businessman wasn't expecting the question, and he blinked a couple of times before he answered. "Soon, I think. I smell the makings of war. I hear the British are going to quarter Hessian mercenaries in Frederick Township. This indicates to me that the British are undermanned and are well aware of that fact. If they think that German colonists will be less hostile to occupation by German troops, they are sorely mistaken."

"'I think you're right," Townsend affirmed. "British General Gates has occupied Boston with four regiments of troops, and the Bostonians are still refusing to pay for all that tea they dumped in the harbor. People are getting shot there, you know. Some of our politically active colleagues are going to convene a congress in Philadelphia, and I don't think the British are going to like that, either."

The elderly German looked behind himself and scanned the room to assure that no one else was present to overhear what he was about to say. He leaned over and spoke to Townsend in a voice that was almost a whisper. "Mr. Carroll of Carrollton is going to that convention. He told me that he expects they will call for an organized armed militia to oppose British military enforcement of the Coercive Acts. I fear the British will treat the colonial representatives and their militia roughly, which will foment even more hostility."

Townsend had wrapped the fine silverware in felt sleeves and carefully placed it in a large polished wooden box, which he presented to his customer. "Will you join me for lunch, Herr von Stueffel? It seems we might have a lot to talk about."

"Thank you, no," the German said. He replaced his hat so he could accept the box with both hands and turned to leave the shop. "The new moon is still very dark, and so I must get to the inn at Ellicott Town before nightfall."

Townsend was perplexed by this comment. "Say again, Sir? What about the moon?"

The German turned back and smiled. "With all this merchandise and newly won money on my person, I wouldn't want to get caught on the Frederick Turnpike after dark. This is the time of month that *Black Yack* and *Spotty Yoe* lurk in the night!"

Townsend chuckled. "I wasn't aware that Black Jack had such a predictable modus operandi. And I though he just bothered the Brits and their Tory collaborators."

"As you very well know, Mr. Townsend, we in the trades all collaborate with the British, whether we want to or not. It's a necessity for remaining in business. How can *Black Yack* possibly know which of us truly is or truly isn't sympathetic to the plight of the Colonials? I wouldn't dare take a chance!"

"I understand," Jonathon Townsend said with a twinkle in his eye. "It's been most pleasurable talking to you today, Herr von Stueffel. And thank you for your patronage. Godspeed on your journey home."

Von Stueffel left, and Townsend returned to his back parlor to reread the documents he had purloined from the British major. One page included the signatures of every alderman in Frederick Town assenting to the quartering of Hessian troops at community expense. The enlisted troops would stay in an unused warehouse near the Frederick Turnpike; the officers would be sheltered and fed in the homes of prominent families of the township. The papers acknowledged that dissenters to this policy would be treated as traitors to the Crown. Jonathon Townsend shuddered as he seethed.

The shopkeeper's ire was interrupted by the sound of the Port Authority's bell, which always sounded loudly to announce the pending dockage of a merchant ship. Townsend closed his shop, saddled Joe Longshanks, and rode three blocks over to the port. He was surprised to see a Spanish galleon being moored to the quay; it had been decades, if ever, since such a vessel had come into Baltimore Port, because the British were perennially at war with Spain. In fact, they had wrested Florida from the Spanish only ten years before. Townsend knew that no one aboard that ship would be interested in glassware, silver settings, furniture or bolts of cloth, but he wandered over to the point of debarkation to find out what such a ship was doing in an unquestionably hostile port.

The Spanish ship's Captain and his officers walked down the gangplank and were escorted across the quay to the Royal Customs Office by a contingent of British marines. No enlisted crewmen were allowed to debark the ship at this time.

Jonathon Townsend dismounted from his horse and waited with the gathering crowd of merchants, innkeepers and prostitutes to see what was going to happen. It was almost noon, and he knew that bureaucrats would soon be filing out of the Customs Office to go to lunch. He hoped he would see somebody he recognized that would know what was going on and, better yet, would share that knowledge with him. A clerk named Crowley stepped out of the door precisely at twelve o'clock, and Townsend led his horse directly into the officious little man's path.

"I say, Crowley, I'll share a couple of pints with you if you'll share what's going on with those Spaniards with me."

"Fair enough, Mate," the ruddy-faced civil servant said, grinning.

Townsend tethered his horse and followed Crowley into the quayside pub.

Before the first pint of ale was consumed, Townsend had learned that the galleon had been bound from Hispaniola to Cuba, and had been blown severely off course by a very early summer storm. The currents and breezes were such that the captain couldn't tack his cumbersome ship back down the Florida coast, and the British Fleet wouldn't allow him to get near San Augustine or Charleston. He had a cargo of workhorses consigned to Havana, and when he ran out of provisions for them he threw them overboard along the Carolina coast. He could not follow the currents and winds back to Spain before his crew starved to death, so he put in to Chesapeake Bay in hopes of finding a charitable haven that would allow him to buy provisions. He just happened to have a fortune in gold and silver in his hold.

"So what did the King's Agent decide to do," Townsend asked.

"The Spaniard can provision his ship, of course. We're not at war with Spain this week, so why not take his gold. Everyone in Baltimore will benefit from it. That kind of money gets spread around, you know; we call it trickle-down effect. The Customs Master advised him to go to Connleigh Provender, because Mr. Connleigh has a warehouse full of flour just in from the Ellicott mills that can be carried across the quay to his ship in the next twenty-four hours. In these hard times, what with the Colonial discontent and all, this is a financial godsend for Baltimore Port.

Even the crew is going to be allowed ashore; we might as well garner their pocket change while were at it!"

Jonathon Townsend paid for Crowley's ale and walked out of the pub to retrieve his horse. He suddenly found himself thinking like Black Jack. *The Spanish Captain will pay in hard currency to deplete Mr. Connleigh's stores of flour. Mr. Connleigh is therefore going to have to go up the Frederick Turnpike to the mills at Ellicott to order more flour. I'm certain he's a Tory, so he really needs to meet up with me on that road!*

Townsend smiled to himself and walked across the quay with his quiet brown stallion in tow. He saw an old black man fishing off the quay's concrete bulwark and called out to him.

"Say, Ned! Are you catching any fish today?"

Ned was a white haired freedman who was a fixture on the quay. "No, Suh, Mr. Townsend; ain't had a bite. Prolly cuz I ain't usin bait. Got a real shiny hook, though. I keeps hopin I'll get lucky."

Townsend laughed and handed him a copper coin. "Here, Ned, get yourself some kippers for that hook."

The old man chuckled. "I don't know if I'd wanna risk fishin wit dem kippers, or just eat em outright. Bait don't always get you a fish, you know, Mr. Townsend." He tucked the copper into his pocket and kept his fishing line exactly where it had been all morning.

"Say, Ned. Would you do me a favor for a silver coin?"

The old man looked up to the horseman and smiled broadly. "I'd do you a favor for nothing, Mr. Townsend, so long as it ain't too illegal."

Townsend grinned. "You know everybody, Ned, so you must know someone who knows what's going on over there at Connleigh's." He pointed across the quay at the Connleigh

Provender sign. "Do you think you could find out when Mr. Connleigh is going go to Ellicott to purchase more flour after that Spanish captain buys him out?"

"Yes Suh, Mr. Townsend. Fact is, I already knows. Old Jeddah, his African coachman, gonna pick him up right there in front of his warehouse at dusk tomorrow evenin and drive him straight up the Frederick Turnpike to Ellicott Town."

Jonathon Townsend's mouth dropped open in amazement. "How on earth did you deduce that, Ned?"

"I been setting here fishin for thirty years, Mr. Townsend, and I observes a lotta folks' habits. Mr. Connleigh can't stand a empty warehouse; he allus waits till the last bag of flour is loaded and then makes a bee-line for the mills to order more. It'll take em all day to load that ship tomorrow, and then Mr. Connleigh gonna hit the Frederick Road arunnin. Say, it'll be Friday; so his daughter will go along wit him. She allus goes if it's Friday, cuz she doesn't study her music on weekends. Course, they won't go if it's dark or rainin, but tomorrow the moon will be shinin bright!"

"What has the moon got to do with whether they go or not, Ned?"

"Oh, Mr. Townsend! Everybody know if you go on the Frederick Road in the dark, Black Jack the Highwayman and Spotty Joe will rob you blind! But God can see those spawns of Satan in the moonlight, so they don't dare venture out for mischief when He be alookin."

Black Jack's alter persona suppressed a triumphant guffaw and handed old Ned a silver coin that could buy enough kippers to last a month.

Leading Joe Longshanks, Townsend turned away from his philosophic informant on the bayside bulwark and nearly stumbled over a child-sized person who had been standing behind him. "Excuse me, little…" Townsend caught himself in mid-sentence as he realized he was balancing himself on a very small mustachioed adult male who was wearing a yellow Spanish sailor's hat and a little goatee.

The little man scrambled to keep his balance and stepped back in embarrassment. "Please forgive me, *Señor*. I was admiring your fine horse. He is quite certainly the most beautifully, how you say in English, *conformed*, horse that I have ever seen!"

"Well, thank you, young man. I have to agree with you on that point."

The horseman focused on the Spaniard to assure that he was indeed a young man, and was convinced by the smoothness of his bronze skin that he was youthful, and by the mustache and goatee that he was male. The fellow was no taller than five feet, and he could not have weighed more than seven stone. He appeared to be of mixed race, perhaps Spanish and Indian or African.

"You seem to know about horses," Townsend said to him. "Have you worked with them in your country?"

"In Hispaniola I have trained many horses, *Señor*, but none so *guapo* as this. He is truly beautiful. I can tell by looking at him that he can run faster than the wind. Let me come to your *casa* and take care of him for you."

Townsend momentarily forgot about the Frederick Turnpike, overbearing Englishmen, and thoughts of revolution. He owned a fast horse, and he knew it. He had galloped Joe Longshanks on the muddy turnpike at breakneck speed, and the sturdy colt had come out of each exercise none-the-worse-for-wear. But could he beat those horses at Annapolis or Newmarket? The ones owned by British governors and generals and rich Tory merchants? Townsend could never know until he found a jockey that weighed seventy pounds less than he did. And now, suddenly and unexpectedly, he was looking at one who was asking for a job.

"What is your name, young man? And how is it that a horseman ends up in the Spanish Navy, and even worse, finds himself in Baltimore with no horses?"

"My name is Rafael. I'm not in the Navy, *Señor*. I went with the horses that I had spent years training. We were supposed to go to Havana to a cavalry regiment, but we got blown out to sea! When we ran out of food for the horses, the captain was going to feed them to the crew! But the sailors didn't want to eat those beautiful creatures! We persuaded the officers to let them swim to freedom in the Carolinas." Tears formed in Rafael's eyes as he recounted this part of the story. "There were dangerous reefs along the shoreline, so we couldn't get too close. My babies were thrown into the sea and had to swim for their lives. They were malnourished from lack of grain, but they were high-spirited and wanting to live. I believe in my heart that every one of them made it to shore. God loves horses, *no es verdad*? They have to be alive now in the Carolinas and eating green grass along the beaches. Please let me come and take care of your horse, *Señor*. I need to be with horses. I can sleep with him wherever he lives. I'm little, and I don't eat much."

Jonathon Townsend mounted his horse and extended his hand to the little Spaniard. "Throw away that silly hat and climb up here behind me," he said as he pulled the smiling Rafael up. "You may not eat much, but I've got a big bite for you to chew."

As he turned Joe Longshanks toward home, the horseman and the Spaniard heard old Ned call out from the bulwark. "Let me know when you race that there hoss, Mr. Townsend. I has some silver what I wants to bet on him!"

***

Friday, June 24, 1774

The badly rutted section of the Frederick Road was brightly illuminated by a glorious full moon in a cloudless sky. Black Jack the Highwayman decided this was good, because the coachman would be able to see the hazardous surface and would slow down well in advance of running over it. And there was the element of surprise; Black Jack and Spotty Joe had never before struck on a moonlit night. The horseman cloaked himself in the darkness of a shady oak motte and was delighted that he could see far up the turnpike and would be able to discern which coach he wanted to stop well before it got to him. His target appeared just as old Ned had predicted.

Jack sat balanced in Joe's saddle with a pistol in each hand, and Joe responded flawlessly to his rider's knee commands. He stepped out in front of the coach as it slowed to a crawl over the ruts and pointed both pistols at the flabbergasted coachman.

"Stop the coach and put yer hands behind yer haid," he shouted.

In fifty years of driving for the Connleighs, old Jeddah had never been so frightened. His eyes were as wide as saucers as he obeyed the highwayman's command. "I ain't armed, Suh," he said with a shaky voice. "Please don't shoot nobody!"

"How about Mr. Connleigh? He gotta gun?"

This question of course clued the merchant in the coach that he was a designated target. He popped the door open and stepped out onto the road with his hands outstretched to show that he was not a threat. Mr. Connleigh was a robust man in his fifties, impeccably dressed, and not the slightest bit amused with his plight. "I have no weapon," he stated. "I have no desire to duel with the likes of you, Sir."

"I'll take yer purse, Sir," the highwayman said with indifference to his victim's slur. "And yer wallet. Hand them up carefully."

"Here is my purse," the gentleman said as he held up the leather bag of coins by its string. "There is only ten pounds. I don't have a wallet."

"What do you mean, you don't have a wallet?" Black Jack was so surprised that he forgot to fake his brogue. He quickly recovered his composure and his villain's vocabulary. "How do ye speck to do bizness without no foldin money?"

"Surely you know about banks, Jack. Mr. Ellicott will charge my account and credit his own at the bank in Baltimore when the flour is delivered. I wouldn't be so stupid as to carry such sums around in negotiable tender. I doubt that you would either."

"Ye be real smart, Govner. Cept bringing yer daughter on a dangerous road at night ain't too wise, now, is it. Hey, li'l Lassie! Come on out of that coach and gimme yer handbag!"

"Stay where you are, Mary Anne!" the merchant ordered boldly.

Jack lifted his left hand and fired his pistol just over the top of the carriage. The report was deafening, and the echo resounded up and down the turnpike as disturbed birds flew from their roosts in nearby trees. Old Jeddah, sitting in the driver's seat, covered his ears and buried his head between his legs in fear. Jacks ears were ringing, and he knew the blast had the same effect on the Connleighs. He dropped the pistol into his saddlebag and pulled another loaded one out and cocked it with his thumb. "The next shot goes through the coach door and through anybody that's still in it, do ye savvy?" He continued to point his right hand's pistol at Mr. Connleigh's chest.

Black Jack got a glimpse of a well-turned ankle as Mary Anne Connleigh quickly stepped down out of the coach. She wore a full-sleeved dress with hems and petticoats that brushed the ground, and a large gold locket hung from a chain on her exquisite neck. Her hair was blonde and long, her face was heartstoppingly beautiful, and if the glare from her eyes could kill, Jack would be dead.

"You are a common cad, Black Jack Scallywag!" she yelled in a voice that Jack found heavenly. "Father has given you his money, and you have nearly scared poor Jeddah to death. Here, take my handbag! Maybe you can use some face powder for your next crime spree!"

"Just hand me the locket, Lassie," he said sternly.

Even in the moonlight Jack could see the girl's face blanch perceptibly.

"Please, Sir, not my locket. It's my mother, you see."

"I said give it to me."

The girl's lips began to quiver as she reached back behind her neck to release the clasp of the chain that held the locket. With her hands up and behind her head, Jack could get a notion of her lithe shape. Mary Anne Connleigh was the most beautiful human female he had ever encountered in his life, and he almost wondered aloud why he had never seen her around the town of Baltimore before this moment. She began to cry as he took the locket from her hand.

Jack flipped the cover open and saw a large cameo of a beautiful woman whom Mary Anne greatly resembled. He had to pry his eyes from it to make sure that Mr. Connleigh was not going to try to rush him. Mr. Connleigh simply put his arms around his daughter and looked up with pleading eyes.

"Have a heart, Jack, please. Her mother gave her that cameo on her deathbed. It's the only likeness we have of her."

Jack closed the cover and held the locket by its chain out over his horse's shoulder for her to reach. "You'd better put it back on and get back in the coach," he said quietly.

"So you do have a heart, Jack!" Mr. Connleigh said as he allowed himself to smile and take a step closer to Spotty Joe.

"*You* won't, if ye come any closer," Jack said as he again lowered his pistol toward the merchant's chest.

Mr. Connleigh stepped back. "I was just looking at your horse's conformation, Jack. He's really an eye catcher, you know. Too bad you monkeyed with his pedigree, what with those horrible spots and all. He might have been a great racehorse otherwise."

"Never you mind his pedigree, Guvner! Old Spotty Joe takes me where I want to go as fast as I need to get there. So git back in yer coach and be mindin yer own pedigree. Git on yer way, and be takin care of that purty lass."

Jack waited with threatening pistols for Mr. Connleigh to follow his daughter into the carriage and shut the door. He was startled when the merchant stuck his head out of the window.

"Before we go, Jack, take a look in the carriage boot. There's something there that you might want to make use of."

Perplexed, Jack guided Spotty Joe to the back of the coach and leaned over to open the trunk that was attached to the rear chassis. He was amazed to find three brand new rifled muskets still in their protective felt casings. He lifted them out one at a time and inserted them barrel first into his large canvass saddlebag. As he did he retrieved the gentleman's purse with the intention of giving it back to him, but when he dropped the trunk lid, the resulting noise sounded like a whip snap and the carriage bounded off into the moonlight.

Jack decided not to push his luck by running after the carriage, because, for all he knew, a brigade of redcoats could be coming over the hillocks from any direction at any moment. Instead, he went back to his base in the abandoned tobacco field and carefully stored the muskets with the others that he had accumulated there. He smiled with satisfaction in the realization that his secret Baltimore militia regiment would be as well armed as any the British could field against them.

While Jack was washing Spotty Joe's disguise off of Joe Longshanks' shiny brown coat, he reminded his horse that Mr. Connleigh had been wrong about adulterating his pedigree. "The stewards at Annapolis are going to swoon when they certify you for the races in July, Joe. And the lords and ladies are going to swoon when Rafael rides you over the finish line. Do you know anything about women, Joe? I think I'm in love."

***

Thursday, July 14, 1774

Jonathon Townsend and Rafael each rode one of the Townsend riding horses and Joe Longshanks followed behind on a lead line. The trip to Annapolis had taken the better part of Wednesday, and after a good night's rest at an inn that catered to horsemen, the two men spent Thursday morning accomplishing things that had to be done in order to participate in the races.

A very thorough and well-organized Jockey Club had taken root in Annapolis in 1750, and the ministrations of the stewards were authoritative and strictly adherent to protocol. Every horse had to be approved for pedigree and soundness by the stewards before entering a race, and the race had to be officially certified before a trophy or wager could be claimed. When the stewards saw Joe Longshank's pedigree papers, they reacted as Jonathon Townsend had predicted; Joe Longshanks was a son of the famous British Thoroughbred, Eclipse, and they fell over each other to take a look at him. Townsend was assured that he could run Joe Longshanks in any race he desired to enter.

The race conditions were listed in a pamphlet that had been printed at considerable expense by the Jockey Club, and Townsend, von Stueffel, and a horse enthusiast named Caton, from Catonville, sat in the Public House annex to the inn drinking ale and studying the specifications. Their jockeys sat together at the next table drinking ale at their employers' expense and playing mind games with each other.

"So we will go a mile and a half in race three on Friday," Mr. Caton said with finality. "We need to drum up some other entrants, so the wager purse will be high. I think I can persuade my cousin Will Ellicott to enter, though his horse is not as well bred as any of ours. Let me say, Mr. Townsend, that I had doubts about the veracity of your animal's pedigree until I saw it with my own eyes. I am so excited about racing against such a fine animal that I'm chomping at my own bit. I'm sure Will is going to want to vie against him, too."

"I know of two owners who ought to enter in this race," von Stueffel said with a sly grin. "I will contact them tonight and bring them 'round to the paddock tomorrow. This is going to be a dream race, and I think my horse, *Erlkoenig*, is going to surprise you all. The more entries he can beat, the better!"

"That will make six horses in the race, then," Townsend said, "if the others agree to our challenge. I'm sure Joe Longshanks will make a good race of it. Now, I think we ought to retire early, before our jockeys get too much ale in their heads. I want mine to be thinking clearly on the track tomorrow."

Mr. Caton laughed. "Wisely put, Mr. Townsend. Let's be off to bed, then. But before we go, since this may be the last time we three are alone together here in Annapolis, let me tell you two gentlemen about an important meeting." He leaned over the table and spoke very quietly. "In anticipation of the Colonial Congress in Philadelphia in September, some of us from Maryland are going to assemble at my home in Catonville next Tuesday evening. It is paramount that you two supporters of citizens' rights be there for strategic input. It is also imperative that the fact of this meeting be kept utterly secret."

Townsend and von Stueffel were each surprised to realize that the other was part of a dangerous common conspiracy. Both nodded solemnly to Mr. Caton, and then they all smiled jauntily in acknowledgement of their potentially fatal complicity. The gentlemen gathered their inebriated little jockeys, sent them to the stables to sleep with their charges, and then retired to their quarters in the inn.

***

Friday, July 15, 1774

The racing fields were located just outside Annapolis on the farm of a wealthy English planter. Tents were set up along the raceway, and the wealthy horse owners had long tables set with elegant silver and glassware where they could sit with their ladies during the post parades. Liveried servants swarmed about the tents serving champagne and exotic foods to the formally dressed crowd of racing enthusiasts. There won an enclosed paddock between the horse barns where the horses could be observed as they were being saddled. It was at this saddling paddock that the owners would make their final entries into the races. At this paddock also were booths where bookmakers posted the betting odds as horses were entered; the odds changed regularly according to the amount of money that was wagered on any given horse in any given race.

Jonathon Townsend, dressed in his finery, was nearly bowled over by the elegance of the scenario. He went to the barn to check on Joe Longshanks and Rafael and then walked to the paddock, all the while imagining that Ascot in England could be no more splendid than this. He stopped at a bookmaker's stand and bet six shillings on his horse for old Ned, as he had promised he would. He then shortly found Mr. Caton, Caton's cousin Will Ellicott, whom he knew, Herr von Stueffel, and a grandly uniformed British general sipping champagne and chatting by the paddock fence.

"Mr. Townsend, please meet General Sir Arthur Milcaster," von Stueffel said by way of introduction. "The general has come from Virginia to race, and has entered his fine horse to compete against us."

The general shook Townsend's hand vigorously. "I understand that I am having an opportunity to run against an Eclipse colt. How absolutely invigorating, Mr. Townsend! It should make a fine race, if I may say so. Do we know how many horses are in the race yet?"

"Six, I believe," von Stueffel replied. "Ah, here comes the other entrant now."

As they all turned to see who else was coming, Townsend felt his heart skip a beat. Mr. Connleigh was stepping into their midst, and his beautiful daughter was holding his arm. Townsend would have been less surprised, and less anxious, if the Devil himself had joined the group.

Von Stueffel again made the introductions. Townsend shook Mr. Connleigh's hand, doffed his fashionable beaver hat and bowed as he said *"Enchante!"* to the daughter. She returned his smile, but had a quizzical look in her eyes.

"Have we not met before, Mr. Townsend?"

"I am certain that we haven't met before, Miss Connleigh. I could never forget meeting someone as lovely as yourself."

"You flatter me, Mr. Townsend," she said merrily as she blushed and averted her eyes."

"Come, Come. We need to talk horses before the races start," Mr. Connleigh said abruptly. "I suggest we circumvent the bookmakers and each put twenty Pounds in a pool, winner takes all."

Jonathon Townsend gulped when he heard the size of the bet, but he had always wanted to play with the big boys, and he shook hands around the group of owners in acceptance of the wager. He had saved enough money from his other, less savory, avocation to pay the sum if he lost, but he had no expectation of losing.

"Owning an Eclipse offspring is a special thing," Mr. Connleigh added. "Would you mind, Mr. Townsend, if I looked at the pedigree? It would be an honor simply to hold such a document in my hands."

"With pleasure, Sir," the handsome shopkeeper replied. He reached into his breast pocket, extracted the papers, and handed them to the wealthy merchant. The general and Will Ellicott sided up to Connleigh to look over his shoulder at the document. They were all horse lovers, and their faces showed pleasure as Connleigh read horse names that went back to the Godolphin Arabian. They also knew that they were about to lose the bet they had just made. The old expression from England, "Eclipse first and the rest nowhere," was well known to racing fans around the world, and Eclipse's offspring were carrying on the tradition.

"Amusing yourselves over death warrants again?" A newcomer insinuated himself into the crowd and sidled up very close to Mary Anne Connleigh. Again Jonathon Townsend felt his heart skip a beat. The newly arrived officer's left arm was tucked into a sling beneath his red coat, and his left sleeve hung empty at his side. The breast of his uniform was covered with medals.

"Oh, Hedley, you're always so amusing," Miss Connleigh gushed with her musical voice. "Mr. Townsend's horse is by Eclipse himself, and we are getting to see the pedigree! Father's horse is going to run against him."

"Oh, tally ho," the officer replied with supercilious indifference.

"Gentlemen, some of you have not met my son," the general said to the group with booming pride. "Mr. Townsend, Mr. Caton, meet Hedley Milcaster, recently decorated for meritorious service to His Majesty and just yesterday promoted to colonel!"

"A pleasure to meet you, Colonel," Townsend said as he extended his hand. "I see that you are injured. Mending well, I hope."

The colonel offered a limp handshake and a bored expression in return. "I sustained a trifling injury when my horse rolled over on me during a skirmish with highwaymen on the Frederick Road. My hand will be back to normal soon, I'm sure." He turned to Mary Anne Connleigh with a woeful expression, and she returned a sympathetic smile.

"Hedley was outnumbered three to one, but was about to make short shrift of Black Jack's gang when his horse fell," General Milcaster announced with unveiled admiration for his son. "Those brigands will think twice before they molest anyone else."

"I'm glad to hear we can travel safely on that road now," Mr. Connleigh said with a straight face. "Come now, the first race is starting."

As they walked to the tents, Jonathon Townsend came to some startling conclusions. *The Connleighs had not reported their encounter with Black Jack three weeks before, otherwise Hedley would have known that Black Jack the Highwayman was still operating with impunity and would have been too embarrassed to shoot off his mouth. Connleigh was a rich and important man who was in tight with the British, but he had to be a Colonial sympathizer. Sir Arthur Milcaster and Hedley Milcaster were British officers who would hang them all in a twinkling if they suspected their ties with revolutionaries. Hedley was hot to become intimate with Mary Anne, and that was too horrible a thought to even imagine! The Connleighs are going to figure out who accosted them on the Frederick Road sooner or later, and that is going to make it very difficult to get approval as a suitor.* He sat down at Caton's table to watch the first race and lost himself in thought.

When the second race was called to post, Townsend went with the others to the fence to watch the horses cross the finish line and began to experience nervousness about his own race. He turned and walked to the paddock to help with the saddling of his horse for the third race. Rafael and a hired groom were waiting there with Joe Longshanks.

"He's really ready," Rafael said with a grin as the groom legged him up onto the prancing colt. "Your friends are going to be amazed at how badly we beat them." He walked Joe in a tight circle until the other five horses were mounted and ready to proceed. At the sound of the bugler calling them to post, the six competitors filed out of the paddock onto the track.

The post parade was the first opportunity for the public to study the horses in motion, and the public was impressed. Particularly, the owners of the other five horses in the race followed Joe Longshanks long-strided gait with expressions of pending doom.

Mr. Connleigh frowned in thought as he concentrated on the big brown Thoroughbred. "I would swear I've seen that horse somewhere before."

"I have ridden him at leisure down on the Baltimore quay," Townsend said matter-of-factly. "Perhaps you noticed him there."

"I must be getting senile," the merchant answered in a perturbed tone. "How can I not recall where I saw a creature with perfect conformation!"

At that moment the starting gun fired and the horses came charging up the straightaway. When they arrived at the large oval that comprised the circular portion of the track, there was a mile to go and Joe Longshanks was already six lengths ahead of the others. The crowd was cheering for their favorites, but the gentlemen who owned the contenders in the race stood in slack jawed awe as Jonathon Townsend's big brown Thoroughbred left the others a half-furlong behind.

Even the self-enamored Hedley Milcaster eagerly pumped Townsend's hand in congratulations. "I say, Old Chap! That horse could outrun the infamous Spotty Joe! Perhaps I could borrow him one day for a challenge on the Frederick Road!"

Townsend cringed from the remark as he glanced over to Mr. Connleigh. The wealthy merchant simply raised an eyebrow and smiled.

One by one the owners of the horses who had challenged Joe Longshanks honored their wagers. General Milcaster, Will

Ellicott, Mr. Caton, and Mr. Connleigh paid their debts with Pound Notes, which was fortunate for Jonathon Townsend; otherwise the hundred Pounds Sterling would have rendered his purse too heavy to conveniently carry. Townsend surprised them all when he announced that he must be on his way back to Baltimore.

"Surely you will dine with us before you depart," Mary Anne Connleigh cooed.

"No, I cannot," the ecstatic winner replied with palpable regret. "There's so much walking for Joe Longshanks, you see. His sire had only to travel around England, but Joe must face the entirety of His Majesty's North America. I want him to have a less arduous travail, so he must sleep in his own cozy quarters in Baltimore this evening."

"Perhaps some other time then, Mr. Townsend." Blonde curls flowed about Mary Anne's shoulders as she turned and walked toward her father's table with her hand daintily tucked into Colonel Hedley Milcaster's right arm. She looked back to toss an afterthought; "Be careful on the road with that heavy purse, Mr. Townsend; old Black Jack might be hunting you!"

"Don't worry, Miss Connleigh. That scalawag doesn't frighten me at all."

Mary Anne Connleigh stopped walking and gave Townsend a quizzical glance; then she turned again to walk back toward her father's tent hanging onto Hedley's arm.

It occurred to the covert highwayman that he had not used or heard the word "scalawag" in years, except when it was pronounced to him as a rebuke by Mary Anne Connleigh on the Frederick Turnpike a fortnight or so before.

Jonathon Townsend left Annapolis richer, wiser, better connected and more confused about women than he had ever been before. He had not, however, improved his plight vis a vis the King of England's hangman.

***

Tuesday, July 19, 1774

Jonathon Townsend arose early in anticipation of his trip to Catonville. He wanted to depart early enough that he wouldn't have to hurry to arrive before sundown. The First Continental Congress was going to meet in September, much to the consternation of the British in control of North America, and everything he had spent his life working for was going to be at risk because of it. At Catonville he would be meeting with other citizens who, to this point in history, had anonymously guided opposition to overbearing policies of the Crown. Now they would all be aware of one another's identity and would collectively be at risk for retribution from His Majesty's governance. As Black Jack the Highwayman, he had committed capital offences against the Royal Government, and any colleague at this meeting who wavered in loyalty to the cause could send him to the gallows in a twinkling. But this meeting was essential for presenting a solid front for Maryland's representatives to the Congress; those brave people had to go to Philadelphia fully aware of any limits of the political and military resources that backed their demands to their British oppressors.

The doorbell to his shop rang irritatingly, and he looked up from his desk to see a young man entering who served in his underground militia unit. His name was Bud Jones, and he worked around the wharves as a delivery boy.

"I got an urgent message for ye, Cap'n. It's from Mr. Connleigh. His Honor says I gotta wait for yer reply."

Townsend had no earthly idea why the wealthy merchant would want to contact him so early in the day. Visions of Mary

Anne Connleigh suddenly appeared in his head to confuse matters. He broke the seal on the message and read it. The message was printed in exquisite calligraphic script.

"Dear Sir: The meeting you are supposed to attend this evening has had a change of venue. You should instead arrive at my estate at 7PM instant."

"Bud, did Mr. Connleigh give you this message himself?"

"Yessir, Cap'n. He handed it to me his very own self, and he said wit his very own mouff that I gotta bring him an answer from ye. Ye gotta write yer answer on the message and give it back to me, Cap'n, else he won't pay me for my work."

Townsend scribbled, "I shall be in attendance, JT," on the bottom of the message with his quill and handed it back to Bud. He also gave the young man a coin. "Here's a copper for you, Bud. Get this back to Mr. Connleigh as quickly as possible. And don't be late for drill practice Thursday night."

Bud smiled grandly. "Thank ye, Cap'n. I'll be there for certain. We gonna practice with real guns Thursday night, Cap'n? I sure wanna get to feelin equal to them Redcoats, Cap'n."

"Maybe so, Bud. Now be on your way."

Since he didn't have to go to Catonville, Townsend went to the outskirts of Baltimore to watch Rafael exercise Joe Longshanks. Joe worked magnificently, and his owner realized that no one in their right mind would ever place high wagers against him again. But they would pay handsomely to send their mares to an Eclipse-sired stallion, and that could be more profitable than actually racing the big brown colt. Unfortunately, racing was a pastime for the rich and powerful, and a pending revolutionary war could put a damper on the demands for Joe's services. But freedom to conduct business and pursue happiness unencumbered by overseas governance took precedence over

Jonathon Townsend's day-to-day personal concerns, so he spent the rest of the afternoon at his shop preparing for the evening's meeting with fellow dissidents.

The Connleigh Estate was just outside the town of Baltimore, and well-kept arboreal windbreaks shielded the main house from the road that passed by. Passing British patrols would not have suspected the presence of the magnificent Phaeton coaches that belonged to ultra-rich colonists such as Carroll, Ellicott and Caton. Liveried grooms stood about the entrance to the grand home to collect lesser vehicles and mounts from other arriving participants. Inside the house Townsend was surprised to see that the only Connleigh employee present was Bud Jones; the rest of the staff had been dismissed so they could not eavesdrop on the discussions or even identify any participants.

Since there were no servants, no meal could be served. Instead, the men, twelve in all, sat at the large dining table and ate bread and cheese and drank Port wine served by Mary Anne Connleigh. Then, while the men conducted their business, the host's daughter went into the parlor and softly played her piano, which she had purchased in Austria a few months before. The reason Jonathon Townsend had not seen her around Baltimore was that she had been in Europe for the last two years being educated.

Mr. Carroll, who was going to be the group's representative to the Philadelphia Congress, presided at the meeting. There were hundreds of grievances against the British that had to be discussed and parsed into a few succinct demands. It was made clear to all present that treasonable revolutionary intent was not the purpose of the Congress. Most of them were British citizens with strong ties to the motherland and had no desire to be at odds with the government. Their intention was to negotiate with the Crown to their best advantage from a formidable position of consensus.

"I have assurances from the Foreign Office that Parliament wants no disruption of colonial commerce and will be receptive to reasonable requests from us. The heavy-handed martial law in effect in Boston and New York and the forced quartering of troops in the homes of private citizens are as offensive to the British House of Commons as they are to us. But we must demonstrate that a call to arms in opposition to military oppression is something that we can accomplish. We shall not negotiate from a point of perceived weakness."

"I have a regiment of trained troops that can be rallied for duty with six hours' notice," Jonathon Townsend stated. "I have accumulated an armory to adequately equip them, and the funds to keep them in the field for two weeks. These men train as non-paid volunteers, but if the curfews are enforced because of citizen unrest, I'll have to harbor them overnight on training days, and they'll have to be paid something for their trouble. My source of income for this venture is less than noble and isn't infinite, so it is imperative that the Congress determine a way to fund my regiment and others like it."

Mr. Caton stood and applauded. "Your contribution to our cause is vastly appreciated, Mr. Townsend. Do not regret any revenue sources you have devised, because the British have brought this on themselves. I, for one, am not convinced that King George will accede to demands from the common people, neither from here nor from home. Militias such as yours may be necessary to keep us all from the reaches of the hangman, and we'll just have to find the funds to keep you intact."

"Absolutely correct," Mr. Carroll said. "I will strongly advise the Congress to maintain our militias. And with that, I thank you all for coming and wish you a safe journey home, whether it be tonight or tomorrow. We are in your debt, Mr. Connleigh, for hosting us on short notice and for accommodating those of us who can't travel until the morning."

The hour was late, so those who were staying the night immediately retired to their rooms. Others began to file for the door. Mr. Connleigh approached Townsend as he reached for his hat.

"I'd like a word with you, Mr. Townsend, if you please. Would you join me and Miss Connleigh in the parlor for a few minutes?"

Jonathon Townsend didn't know whether to be joyful or fearful. He quickly accepted the invitation and followed his host into the sumptuous parlor. In spite of the hour, Mary Anne Connleigh appeared as fresh and beautiful as ever.

"Please have another Oporto," Mr. Connleigh offered, and his daughter instantly went to pour him a glass of the excellent vintage.

"So you are in the trades, Mr. Townsend?"

"I have a retail shop, yes, Sir. I'm afraid it's not a very large concern, what with the lack of currency in the colonies these days. I deal in cutlery, antiques, furniture and cloth; that sort of thing."

"I am impressed with the way you do business, Mr. Townsend. I wish you'd come around to my offices sometime this week and take a look at my enterprise. Perhaps we can find some mutually beneficial way to combine our resourcefulness and make a little Sterling before hostilities commence."

Townsend smiled, and accepted the Oporto from Mary Anne. "Speaking of Sterling, that reminds me." He reached into his pocket and pulled out a leather purse. "I found this on the Frederick Road. I believe it belongs to you, Mr. Connleigh."

Mr. Connleigh laughed out loud. "You keep it, Jack! Consider it an advance for a stud fee. Joe's foals won't have spots, will they?"

"Only if they have a night job with me," Jonathon answered with a grin. His grin evaporated when he caught sight of Mary Anne Connleigh's somber expression. "To you, Miss Mary Anne, I solemnly and humbly apologize for my egregious behavior on the Frederick Road. I beg your forgiveness, but if you cannot proffer it, I'll understand perfectly."

Her eyes caught his and did not avert. "You are forgiven, Sir. But I have a question for you."

"Oh, thank you, Miss Mary Anne! I am your humble servant for eternity! What is your question?"

"Hedley's horse didn't fall on him, did it?"

"Miss Mary Anne, I could not impugn the actions of a British officer on the field of battle."

"Jack Townsend, you have answered my question. And for the record, I am now convinced that Hedley is a pretentious fop." She smiled coquettishly. "It would be better to be courted by a scalawag than a fop, would it not?"

GOT YOUR GOAT

Friday Menu had just been certified as fit to race by the track veterinarian and was following his trainer and owner back to his barn to wait for his stakes race later in the evening. The big gray gelding began to act nervous as they approached the shed row.

"Whoa, boy! What's the matter with you?" Al Zimmer said soothingly as he tightened his grip on the lead line. "You gotta stay calm, now, Friday. This is a big race coming up, and I don't want you distracting yourself from your job. What's the matter with you, anyway?"

"Uh-oh," Toad Curley said to Al. "I see the problem. Eunice is gone!"

"Where the hell is she?" Al wondered aloud as he led the anxiously prancing Friday Menu into his stall and removed his halter. "She wouldn't just run away, even if she got untied accidentally."

Toad peered into the stall on the left, where a zebra was peering back at him. "She's not in here with Con Man. Let me see if she went into Tammy Taffeta's stall."

Toad looked into the stall on the right and saw only a bay filly chewing on some alfalfa. There was an owl perched in the rafters above the filly's head. The big bird shifted her position and turned her head nearly backwards as though she, too, was looking for Eunice. Toad continued on down the shed row peeking into each stall, but Eunice, Friday Menu's private nanny goat and very best friend, was nowhere to be seen.

Pablo, Al Zimmer's stable hand, drove up to the barn in Al's pickup and hopped out to unload some bales of alfalfa.

"Hey Pablo, where's Eunice?" the trainer shouted.

Pablo squinted his eyes and looked over at Friday Menu's stall. "She was tied right there when I left to get hay. I haven't been gone ten minutes."

"Well, she's gone now," Al said disgustedly. "Even her rope is gone. Friday's gonna work himself into a conniption. We have to find that damned goat, or he won't be fit to race tonight!"

"I'll drive around and look for her," Toad said as he fished his keys out of his jeans pocket. "I'll go by the security gate first, and make sure nobody has tried to take her off the premises."

Within three minutes Toad was as the gate talking to the two security guards.

"Not one van has left through this gate in the last forty minutes," the bigger guard assured as he checked his exit records. "In fact, only one car has left the grounds, and that was Perry Perkman in his Porsche. Weren't no goat with him in that little car."

"Perry Perkman?" Toad exclaimed with interest. "Say, do you have a copy of tonight's race card?"

"Sure do," the officer replied. He went into his kiosk and retrieved a copy of the program from a stack on his desk.

Toad quickly leafed through it to the evening's feature race, which was a one hundred thousand dollar stakes that would be going to post at nine o'clock. Friday Menu was listed in pole position number three at even odds to win. Concatenation, owned by Perry Perkman, was listed as number nine, at fifteen to one odds.

Ten Horse Tales

"I smell a rat," Toad Curley declared. "The problem is, where does a rat stash a goat if he can't haul it off the premises without getting caught?"

"Maybe the stable boys are going to barbecue it," the cop laughed."

"Not funny," Toad said. "I've got a sixty thousand dollar payoff at stake here."

***

It was rumored around the track that Toad Curley and Al Zimmer were Siamese twins that were joined at the hip at birth, because they were inseparable friends. They were both five feet four inches in height and weighed about a hundred and fifty pounds. In their late twenties, they had sandy hair, muscular shoulders, thin hips and, like most people who are placed astride a horse before they learn to walk, were bowlegged. Actually, they did not know each other until they were assigned to the same Army Special Forces Unit in Iraq. Both men, for personal reasons, had abandoned their equine connections to join the military, had found a *raison d'être* during the challenge of war, and had returned to civilian life together to resume successful careers in horse racing.

Al Zimmer came from a line of accomplished horsemen, and he knew that he would have to work his way up the ranks to be successful. He was hardworking and smart, and he earned an assistant trainer's license by age eighteen. At age twenty he was crushed when his young wife left him because his salary as an assistant trainer wasn't enough to provide the kind of lifestyle she craved. Distraught, he walked off his job and enlisted in the Army. He chose a military program that paid an enlistment bonus, and he saved that money and most of his combat pay during his three-year stint in Iraq. He paired with a buddy whose nickname, Toad, belied his true nature, and they worked hard together at assuring their survival of the war experience.

Carl Curley's father and grandfather had been successful jockeys, and young Carl's only desire was to follow in their footsteps. He had inherited athletic talent, fearlessness and keen horse sense. Unfortunately he also inherited a gourmet's sense of taste, and as he got closer to age twenty, he found increasing difficulty in maintaining an ideal weight for racing. When his weight topped one hundred and twenty pounds, very few racing mounts were offered to him, so he became a seldom-utilized exercise rider at paltry pay. He fasted, exercised and took diet pills, but tipping the scales under the one-twenty line became impossible. One by one the trainers reminded him that he was getting fat as a toad, and one by one they withdrew their demand for his services.

And then a moment of redemption came to Carl "Toad" Curley. A lower echelon trainer named Honker Malone got control of a promising unknown colt named Calliope Jazz, and he wanted to run him in a high-weighted handicap. Several big-time horses from out of state came in to run in the three hundred thousand dollar race, and the best local jockeys that didn't have a quality Texas horse contracted to ride those visiting horses. Carl Curley was an experienced jockey whose heaviness would not exceed the impost for the race, and he solicited the mount from Honker Malone.

Honker was a foot taller than Carl and outweighed him by a hundred pounds. He knew that Carl was as good a thinker as any of the other jockeys, but he wanted assurances about Carl's weight. "Calliope Jazz will have to carry a hundred and twenty-six pounds," he said gravely to Carl. "How much are you weighing right now, at this minute?"

"Under one twenty-six, for sure, Honker. Let's go to the jockey's room and get my gear and check my weight. I want this job, and I'll get you sixty per cent of that three hundred grand if you'll trust me."

As they walked to the jockey's room, they nodded a hello to Perry Perkman, who was chatting with his trainer and a jockey.

"That's the guy you're going to have to beat," Honker said to Carl in a low voice. "With just a hundred and twenty-six on his back, old Calliope should leave Perkman's horse in the dust. I'm gonna love beating that rich little monkey."

With his saddle, helmet, boots and protective vest in hand, Carl Curley showed Honker that he weighed one hundred and twenty-five and one-half pounds. "I'll have to carry a half pound of lead to meet the impost," he said with a grin.

Honker shook his new jockey's hand. "Okay, you're on," he said. "I'll enter tomorrow morning. Will you gallop Calliope for me tomorrow and Friday?"

"You bet," Carl answered enthusiastically. "I'll see you at your barn at sunup!"

"Be sure you don't eat anything but air for the next three days, Carl Curley," Honker added sternly.

***

Carl rode Calliope Jazz two mornings in a row, and professed to his trainer that the horse was ready for his Saturday race. The weight-challenged jockey remained true to his word and ate less than a canary for two days running, and he fought off lightheadedness and a driving temptation to eat by thinking of nothing but the pending race. He was focused, really focused, on his task when he stepped in front of an oncoming Porsche and was nearly run over as the vehicle swerved to miss him. The convertible screeched to a stop and it's driver bounded from the car.

"Holy crap, Curley! Are you okay?" a shaken Perry Perkman shouted as Carl brushed dust from his clothes. "I damned near nailed you! You were walking like your mind was on another planet!"

"I'm alright, Mr. Perkman. You're right; my mind was wandering. Thanks for not killing me."

Perkman playfully jabbed the jockey on the arm. "Glad you're okay. Hey, Curley, I see you're riding for Honker Malone now. What do you think about that nag of his, Calliope-what's-his-name?"

"He's a nice horse, actually. We may have a crack at you tomorrow night, Mr. Perkman."

"I like your attitude, boy. Sorry you're so fat, or I'd have you aboard my stakes contenders in a New York minute."

Carl Curley smiled. He knew Perkman was playing a head game with him. "You'd better have your jock wear his glasses tomorrow, Mr. Perkman. Otherwise he won't be able to see me up there ahead of him."

Perry Perkman laughed and slapped Carl on the back. "You got a sense of humor, Curley, I'll say that for you. But I'm serious; maybe we can do some business soon. Hey, can I buy you lunch? It's the least I could do after almost running you over. Let me give you a little spin in my mo-tor-car."

Mo-tor-car was an inference to Mr. Toad in the tale, *Wind in the Willows*, and Carl Curley, a twenty-year-old jockey who wasn't a Classics reader, didn't pick up on the slur. Instead, he took Perkman's offer as a friendly gesture and accepted it He would end up in the sand, literally, because of his gullibility.

"Have you been to C'est Magnifique?" Perkman asked.

"Never could afford that place," Carl answered. "Do they have any light low-cal stuff? I'm on a four-plus serious diet."

"Oh, sure," Perkman avowed. "They have stuff you can eat all day and not get a single calorie."

Carl Curley's stomach sent an overriding message to his reluctant brain: *really good food; rich guy buying.* "Okay, let's give C'est Magnifique a try!" his mouth responded to his gastric urge.

They entered the world-renown French restaurant, and Perkman winked discreetly at the maître d'hôtel. "Lunch for two, Pierre. A quiet table where we can talk business."

"Very good, Monsieur; I have ze perfect table for you." The tuxedoed host led them to a table in a darkened corner of the dining room where the bow-legged peasant in jeans and tee shirt would be least offensive to the sensibilities of his haut couture regulars.

"Remember, I have to keep it light, Mr. Perkman."

"No problem, my boy. We'll start out with a hearts of palm en vinaigrette, and we'll temper the acidity with just a little fois gras. Let's have a split of champagne to go with that, Pierre."

"Are you sure this isn't fattening, Mr. Perkman?" Carl asked as he eyed the plate of exquisitely presented food. "What is fois gras, anyway."

"It's goose. Not a molecule of carbohydrate in it. It's the carbohydrate that puts the weight on ya, you know. Palm is just grass, and champagne is all air. This is heavenly, boy, so have at it!"

The vinaigrette and the champagne cut the richness, but not the flavor, of the goose liver appetizer, and Carl ate a third of a pound of it without feeling full at all. Next came a dozen escargots bourguignon, and he knew better than to use more than two slices of French bread to sop the sauce. He ate the snails very slowly, so the flavor would linger. He finished his champagne, and though he was feeling a little light headed, his stomach didn't feel any fuller.

"We're going to have some coquilles next," Perkman said enthusiastically. "I'll order a bottle of Montrachet to enhance them."

"Which Montrachet do you prefer, Monsieur?" Pierre asked snootily.

"The hundred and fifty dollar one will do fine," the wealthy host declared nonchalantly to impress his guest.

This ploy worked, and Carl's eyes widened at the thought of such a price for a little bottle of white wine. "Uh, what are coquilles?" he asked.

"Sea scallops, and they are being served in a bed of mashed potatoes and smothered with chanterelles and pearl onions in a cream sauce."

"That's way too fattening for me," Carl insisted, but he was salivating when he saw and smelled the dish.

"The Montrachet wine cuts the richness," Perkman said slyly. "That's why it costs so much."

"Oh, good," was Carl's response, and he ate everything on his plate except two token bites of potatoes that any dedicated dieter would leave. He drank over half of the bottle of wine while Perry Perkman grimaced to the heart of his gourmet soul from his perceived waste of it.

"Well, you handled that just fine," Perkman observed. "Let's do a meat course before we do dessert, eh what? What's your favorite red wine?"

"Oh, no more wine for me, Mr. Perkman," Carl responded with a hint of slurring voice. "I'm not even twenty-one yet. Maybe just a little dessert, if you don't mind."

Perkman snapped his fingers to get Pierre's attention and pointed at the dessert-spoon amongst the silver service around his plate; a waiter immediately appeared with two enormous orders of tiramisu.

"This looks like a big milkshake, Mr. Perkman. Anything that looks and tastes this good has got to have a lot of fattening stuff in it."

"Here, Carl, finish off the Montrachet and those calories will be extinguished from your mind in a twinkling. The coffee flavor in there cuts the alcohol, and the lady fingers in there are light and sweet as angels' kisses, are they not?"

Perry Perkman delivered the stuffed jockey to his apartment near the racetrack after four hours of eating and drinking. Carl Curley thought he saw a toad in the mirror before he crashed on his bed and slept until ten the next morning.

Carl woke up with a hangover and a pervasive sense of dread. He wobbled onto his bathroom scale and, when the number one hundred and thirty flashed into his horrified gaze, he said aloud what he had feared from his first waking moment. "I've been had!" He immediately went out and jogged for three hours and felt mounting frustration when the scale continued to register over one-twenty-nine. He took a diuretic even though he felt dehydrated from his workout. Then he went to the track for the inevitable confrontation with Honker Malone.

"My God, Carl! What did you eat since I saw you last, an anchor? What have you done to us, you inconsiderate little bastard? I can't get you replaced with a good jockey this close to the race! This is a three hundred thousand dollar race, and you have screwed me over!"

Carl Curley swallowed hard through a mouth parched dry from medicine-induced water loss. "I'm really sorry, Honker. I really am. But I'm just two pounds over now, Honker, and we're only going a mile. I'll take Calliope Jazz out front and make sure no one catches us. Believe me, I have a score to settle with Perry Perkman; I'll beat his nag, I promise."

The race went off with Carl Curley at two pounds overweight on Calliope Jazz. The colt was fresh and eager to run, and Carl set the pace with Perkman's young colt, Concatenation, two lengths behind. *An extra pound equates to a lost stride in a mile race,* was an adage that hammered through Carl's mind as he came around the second turn to the final stretch. *If I can stay two strides ahead, he'll never catch me!*

But Carl couldn't stay two strides ahead, and the fast-coming Concatenation caught Calliope Jazz at the wire. As both horses were being gradually pulled to a halt after the race, Concatenation's jockey looked over toward the rider he had just overtaken.

"I think I caught you for a photo, Carl. Why on God's earth did you do that to yourself, anyway?"

Carl Curley looked down at the back of his horse's head and realized that he had just ridden his last race. He arrived back at the entrance to the winner's circle as the announcer proclaimed Concatenation winner of the race by a nose. Honker Malone charged out onto the track like an angry bull and snatched the reins from Carl's hands.

"You lost by a wart on his nose, you guzzling slob! You cost me a hundred and twenty grand because you couldn't keep your hungry mouth closed for twenty-four more hours! Get your sloppy ass off my horse, you fat toad, and get out of my sight before I beat those two goddam pounds off of you just for the fun of it!"

"I'm sorry, Honker. I'll make it up to you someday."

"The hell you will," Honker screamed. "You're not going to make a hundred and twenty grand on this track for the rest of your natural-born life! Now go away, Fat Toad Curley, before I just kill you!"

Carl retrieved his saddle and headed for the jockey's room with long strides and lowered head. He had to walk past the winner's circle and a grinning, gloating Perry Perkman.

"Hey, Toad," Perkman shouted at the mortified jockey. "You don't look so happy! Somebody get your goat?"

Carl "Toad" Curley cleaned out his locker and went home. He spent the night packing everything he owned into storage boxes, and early the next morning he enlisted in the Army and a tour in Iraq.

***

For reasons that were abundantly clear, Al Zimmer's barn was known around the racing industry as Zimmer's Zoo.

It had began when Zimmer's filly, a brilliant two-year-old called Tammy Taffeta, made friends with an owl that had cleared her stall of snakes and pigeons. The filly stubbornly refused to work or enter a van if the owl wasn't present. The bird actually roosted on the track floodlights while Tammy Taffeta was exercising or racing.

An old gelded warhorse named Committed Clarence had been claimed and reclaimed on several occasions and was just about due for retirement when Toad Curley brought a young zebra from his grandfather's ranch to the track for veterinary care. Clarence and Con Man took a liking to each other, and the old gelding started to win every race he went in. Al Zimmer decided to keep the zebra so Clarence's recharged attitude would be maintained.

Al also employed a peacock and a large gander as companions for neurotic Thoroughbreds who preferred the friendship of alien species to their equine own. Smaller animals, like cats and rabbits made good companions for horses, but they were imperiled by the owl, who considered them fair game for her own meals. Dogs weren't allowed on the track because they bark at nervous horses and sometimes bite human passersby.

Almost every racetrack had and still has a goat or two for horse company, and Zimmer's Zoo was no exception. Friday Menu was smitten by Eunice, and he was always just a moment away from an anxiety attack when he was taken from her presence to the track to exercise or race.

And now someone had deliberately hidden Eunice away somewhere, and Friday Menu was distraught to the point of mental collapse. The big gray gelding sweated profusely as he paced in his stall. Twice a minute he would hang his head out of the stall doorway and search up and down the shed row for his beloved caprine nanny. Then he would whinny pitifully and return to pacing.

Al Zimmer and Toad Curley were as distraught as Friday Menu. The partnership they had continued after their tour in Iraq had resulted in a successful breeding and training business, and Friday Menu was a race away from becoming their most profitable venture. But suddenly they were a goat away from owning an emotional equine invalid whose career was seriously interrupted by separation anxiety. Eunice had disappeared into thin air.

"I've looked in every dumpster and manure bin within the track's secured area," Toad said to Al as he shook his head dejectedly. "I know it's against ethics to wander through other trainers' barns on race day, but I'm going to do it, Al. If I hear a goat sound in any tack room I'm going to call security and demand entrance. I'm going to look particularly thoroughly around Perry Perkman's barn, because I have a sneaking feeling that he's behind this little caper."

Toad trekked up and down the shed rows looking into each stall. Every closed tack room and feed room door elicited a whistle from him, and he would stop walking for a moment to listen for any response behind the door. Toad was sure that Eunice would respond to his familiar call if she were indeed present behind one of the doors. Toad walked two miles and whistled until his lips hurt, but the only response he got was a snide remark from Perry Perkman, who leaned smirking against his Porsche when Toad passed by.

"You look pretty anxious, Toad," Perkman jeered. "Somebody got your goat again?"

Toad stopped walking and glared at his gloating nemesis. "You know, Perkman, if that horse of yours could run a lick you wouldn't have spent the last four years of your life cheating to get him across the wire ahead of his competition. I'm gonna find my goat, Perkman, and you're gonna end up sucking wind. If you were half a man, or even a tenth of a horseman, you'd tell me where you hid her."

"You're just a poor loser, Toad Boy," Perkman chortled as he climbed into his car. "I don't know a thing about your stupid goat. Maybe the Mexicans are eatin' 'im."

Toad saw smoke rising from an outdoors roasting pit near the grooms' dormitories and ran over to check it out. Several

Hispanic employees were basting a slab of meat in preparation of a Saturday evening feast.

"Cabrito?" Toad asked with trepidation.

"No. Puerco!" the cook replied as he sloshed some more sauce over it. He looked up to Toad and smiled. "We wouldn't be able to eat Eunice, Toad. She's everybody's friend. Besides, we don't like that guy Perkman."

"Do you have any idea where Eunice might be?"

"Sorry, no. But she isn't around the dorms. We already looked for you. Did you look in the dumpster behind the feed store?"

"Yes I did," Toad answered. "I looked in the equipment warehouse, too. I even looked in the cabs of the tractors. Any other ideas?"

"Sorry, no. We'll keep our eyes open for her."

"Thanks," Toad said. "The track opens in an hour. Looks like my horse is going to wash out before we find his nanny."

Toad walked back to the barn, where he found Al and Pablo sponging Friday Menu with cold water. The horse would not stand still in spite of their soothing comments and petting.

"Any luck," Al asked.

"No," Toad answered. "I checked every conceivable place within the secure area, even the dormitories. The trackmen even checked around the light towers for me. Whoever got Eunice must have gotten her outside some way. I'm going to look around the grandstand and concessions before the first race starts, but I'm sorry to say, I think we've had it, Al."

"Well, I'm not going to scratch Friday Menu until they call us to the paddock. We'll keep trying to cool him off until the last minute. Maybe you'll get lucky walking around the grandstand."

Toad walked over to the fence between the backside and the public area of the grandstand. There were track employees starting their jobs in every nook and cranny, and he knew that if a lost goat was anywhere on the premises it would immediately be discovered. He walked past the security guard into the public area, which was now bustling with fans and employees. His heart was heavy with disappointment as he realized that the first race was about to be called; Friday Menu's race was less than three hours away.

Toad chatted with every employee he knew and no one had seen a goat or had any idea where a goat might be tucked out of sight. He walked down to the track and chatted with the outriders who where assembling for the opening ceremonies. They had just ridden over from their own facility and had seen no stray goat. Toad knew that his time had run out when the track's lights came on to illuminate the late fall evening.

The light reflected off the pond in the infield and reminded Toad of the flooding rain that almost engulfed the inner turf course two days before. The water had receded and left a ring of mud and washed-over weeds around the pond. He walked down by the rail in front of the tote board and removed his hat as the Star Spangled Banner began to play. He held his hat over his heart and mouthed the words of the anthem in his mind as he stared into the darkness of the pond, mainly to get his mind off the disappointment of his lost goat and horrible luck.

Oh say, does that Star Spangled Baaaaaa yet wave, o'er the land of the free and the home of the baaaaaa.

"Huh?" Toad shook his head as if to clear his hearing.

"Baaaaaa."

Toad looked at the tote board, which sat on a mound to protect it from flooding from the pond. *What the hell is behind there?* he thought. He vaulted the fence and ran across the track toward the tote board.

"Hey, get back here! Get off that track!" a security guard yelled as be bounded onto the track after Toad. Two outriders spurred their ponies and ran down the track after him also.

Toad easily jumped over the rail between the dirt track and the inner turf track and left his pursuers behind. He cleared the inner rail with equal ease and found himself running in mud as he went behind the tote board.

The area behind the huge display board wasn't visible to the fans in the grandstand area, and therefore was not meticulously maintained like the rest of the track's grounds and gardens. There were waist high weeds growing in the mud around a small copse of mesquite trees and switch willows at the edge of the pond. Toad slogged into the brush when he heard another "baaaaaa."

The security guard gave up his chase when his polished shoes started sticking in the mud. The outriders wouldn't leave their horses, so they remained on the dirt track. All of them just kept yelling, "Hey, you, get out of there!"

Toad found Eunice tied to a mesquite tree. She tried to jump up and hug him when he approached, and got mud all over his clothes.

"I'm glad to see you, too, silly critter," Toad laughed. "Let's get you loose and back to your buddy Friday. He's going to be even happier to see you than I am!"

When Toad stepped out from behind the tote board with Eunice in hand, several people in the grandstand began to cheer. The cop stopped yelling and helped Toad get under the rail with the goat. They walked back across the dirt track and exited through the winner's circle as the entire crowd cheered at the novelty of the opening ceremony. The guard closed the gate and the bugler called the first race to post as Toad Curley led Eunice back to her rightful home and her soon to be relieved best friend.

By the time of the featured race, everyone on the premises knew the story of Friday Menu and the kidnapping of Eunice, and Al and Toad watched their horse come out of the gate as an odds-on favorite. Friday Menu beat Concatenation by seven lengths, and his reward, by special dispensation of track management, was to be joined in the winner's circle by his dear nanny.

"I think I got *your* goat this time," Toad said with a grin as he led Eunice past Perry Perkman into the winner's circle.

REFLECTIONS OF A WARHORSE

The grassy pasture where I was born obviously belonged to somebody important, because no estate in Macedon could have been more beautiful. A clear cool stream tumbled out of a craggy mountainside and meandered through the meadows to a copse of olive trees near the stables where my mother and I lived. Laborers had compartmentalized the long stone barn into stalls, one for each mare and foal, and had covered it with a sturdy thatched roof to protect us from the rains that blew in from the Aegean Sea. Three times a day a smelly red-bearded man who wore a sheepskin loincloth would bring us grain in wooden buckets. Then he would encourage us to go down to the stream to drink, play, and snooze while he cleaned our stalls and replaced the straw bedding. I imagined that this unwashed groom's name was 'Stinky,' and I became quite fond of him when he started brushing me every day and scratching my withers. It was very idyllic, and I had no suspicion that my future life was going to be very different from what I imagined.

When I was about four months old I became aware of the morning monsters that tried to overtake me as I trotted down to the stream at dawn, and in the evenings I could sense more monstrous evilness as I plodded up the field to the safety of my stall. I told my mother about this, but she just snorted and implied that I was being foolish. She reminded me that I was soon to be weaned, which meant that I would be alone for the rest of my life and I'd better toughen up. *Alone with the morning monsters!* I thought. This certainly engendered some anxiety, let me tell you!

One day, when I was six months old, Stinky led my mother out of the stall and locked me inside. I squealed dreadfully as he herded her and the other mares to a pasture far across the stream. I was not mollified by the fact that all the other foals along the shed row were crying, too. It was dark in that stall, but I didn't worry much about the monsters because I was too busy missing my home-prepared meals. Stinky seemed to be sorry for what he was doing to me, because he came into the stall often with handfuls of grain and gentle-voiced comments and patted and hugged me.

After about ten days I wasn't missing my mother as much as I was missing running and playing in the pasture. Stinky seemed to know this, so early one morning he let all of us out for a romp in the open field. My fellow weanlings and I dashed out into the warm morning sunshine and ran gleefully across the pasture toward the stream.

But in moments my joy turned to dread! As I galloped over the grass I looked down to discover that the morning monster was tracking me! My heart pounded as I ran for cover in the shade of the olive copse, and I spent the whole morning cowering there while my stable-mates frolicked in the open pastures. Stinky came down to the copse later in the day to get me, and I nearly ran over him trying to get back to the safety of my stall. Like my mother, Stinky implied that I was very foolish, but he groomed me with loving care anyway. Perhaps he thought I would outgrow my phobias.

Partially because of Stinky's dutiful feeding and grooming, and certainly because of the genetic proclivities of my sire and dam, I grew to become a healthy and sturdy colt. I was big-boned, with a short back, powerful rump and shoulders, and wide feet. I could run like the wind, especially if the monsters were after me. Fortunately, during the cloudy winter months the monsters didn't come out to harass me, so I was able to graze, exercise, and play gamely with the other growing horses. A full year went by, and nothing changed except the seasons, my size and my agility.

One cloudy day in early spring a whole herd of older horses appeared at the stable gates. I had never seen anything like them. They had humans on their backs! And what magnificent humans they were. They wore shirts decorated with furs and colorful feathers, leather skirts lined with bronze plates and open-toed sandals with straps that extended to their knees. Each man carried a spear that was thrice the length of Stinky's shepherd staff. The leader, a swarthy warrior in his early twenties, dismounted and waited for the stable hand to approach. Stinky ran to him, fell to his knees, and bowed his disheveled head to the ground in obeisance.

"Get up and show me what you have here," the leader said gruffly.

Stinky jumped to his feet and waved his arm toward the stalls. "They are all magnificent, Master," he said confidently. "They will pull the king's charioteers over the enemy's ranks as bravely as any war-horses that have ever served him. It is the best crop of yearlings that I have ever raised."

The leader smiled through his trimmed black beard and nodded approvingly. "I like it when they all turn out exceptionally well. Bring them out, and my men will lead them to the training camp."

"Yes, Master! Right away, Master. But there is one colt here that is very special, and you may want to make a cavalry charger of him. His conformation is superb, and he is fast and agile on his feet. The star on his forehead is shaped like a bull, which is a good omen."

"Well, let's have a look at him then," the leader said, returning to his gruff demeanor. "I need such a horse for a special purpose, but he'll have to be perfect."

I watched with amazement as Stinky led the *hipparchos* to *my* stall. He attached a lead line to my halter and paraded me out for the master horseman to look over. I was surprised and pretty flattered that he thought that I was the finest horse in this crop of yearlings, so I set my mind to proving that he was right! Luckily no monsters materialized to disrupt my debut.

"I want you to come to the training camp with this horse," the master said to my groom. "If he turns out to be as good you think he is, life will get better for both of you."

***

Training was certainly different than living in an idyllic pasture. After Stinky fed me every morning before sunup, the horsemaster would take me to a large round pen and make me walk, trot and canter around it until I was sweating like a plow horse. He would throw blankets over my back and dangle ropes over my rump. I got so that I could heed his commands to his satisfaction, and then he'd give me back to Stinky to be bathed, brushed and fed all the hay I could eat. But then one sunny morning the *hipparchos* decided to get on my back. My career took a divergent turn, and I got named.

When the horsemaster placed the blanket over my back, I was not surprised. He jumped up and threw his leg over me, sat into the blanket, and took the reins from Stinky. I looked down when Stinky stepped away, and that's when I realized that the biggest monster I had ever encountered was about to envelope me and the man sitting on my back. I reacted by lowering my head and bucking violently with my rear end, and the *hipparchos* was launched into a trajectory that sent him head first over the fence and into a mud hole. I raced around the round pen looking for a way out, and Stinky had to dive out of my way to avoid being trampled. Some friends of the horsemaster who had been watching through the fence burst into raucous laughter at the sight of their colleague groveling in the mud, but that ended abruptly when I jumped over the fence into their midst. As they scattered to get out of my way, some of them slipped into the same mud hole, and my blanket flew off on top of them. Then the *hipparchos* started to laugh hysterically at his mud-covered friends.

Terrified, I ran back to my stall, and shortly the chagrined groom came in to secure me and remove my bridle. Stinky was shaking from fear, but I paid him no heed, because I had no concept of the pecking order that humans establish in their relationship with one another. Stinky cowered beside me when the *hipparchos* and his friends walked up to the stall door and peeked in.

One brown-headed young friend was incredibly handsome, but he spoke with a slight lisp. He was still snickering when he commented to the horsemaster, who was wiping mud off his face. "You sure picked a crazy one, Ptolemy! Old Philhippos gonna demote you to *peltast second class* when you present him with this bull-headed colt!"

The *hipparchos* smiled broadly. "Yeah, Hephaestion, but did you see how easily he jumped over that fence! No horse at this facility has ever jumped out of there before! This horse has talent, my friend, and I intend to develop it. Hey, you, groom, bring him back out to the pen." He turned to his friends and grinned. "He won't be bucking me off again; I won't get surprised twice."

Stinky replaced my tack and the blanket and led me, with both of us trembling, back into the round pen. He held my head tightly as the horsemaster remounted.

"Okay, you, let him go."

I stood there quivering as Stinky stepped away. Then I sensed the monster again. I stood up on my hind legs and pawed the sky with my front feet. I could feel the man on my back move his body forward against my neck to keep his balance. Then I saw the monster, bigger than ever, rising up from the bowels of the earth to envelope me! I instantly planted my front feet and simultaneously bucked my rump, and Ptolemy the Horsemaster was instantly airborne over my head. He landed with a thud in the soft dirt, and again I leapt the fence and galloped to my shady abode where no monsters dwelt. Stinky ran out through the gate after me while the master's friends laughed their heads off one more time.

"Ptolemy, you have the reflexes of a snail," Hephaestion said chidingly. "Get that horse back out here and let me show you how to ride him!"

So one more time Stinky led me into the pen and held my head. Ptolemy gave Hephaestion a leg up and again there was a rider on my back. This time I lowered my head and bucked first, and Hephaestion leaned back and held on. As he did so, I suddenly thrust myself up and forward with my front legs and he tumbled over my tail. He lit in the dirt flat on his butt and with

Ten Horse Tales

a look of utter incredulousness on his face. The *hipparchos* fell to his knees laughing while Stinky ran out of the round pen gate after me on my way to my stall.

Another group of mounted men unexpectedly appeared between the round pen and the stables, and the laughter stopped. Ptolemy and Hephaestion scrambled to their feet and bowed deeply from the waist toward the lead rider. Stinky stopped running and prostrated himself flat on the ground with his face precariously close to a plop of dung.

King Philhippos was lighter complexioned than his subjects. His brown beard was graying, and he was splendidly attired in the garb of a Greek cavalry officer. He sat magnificently and gently astride his horse, which should be expected from a man whose name means *horse lover*. He appeared amused as he addressed the horsemaster. "You seem to be having a mirthful day, Ptolemy, though I am perplexed as to why the two best *hipparchoi* in the Macedonian Cavalry find it funny to be unhorsed. Was that a Pegasus that I saw fly out of here?"

"No, Sire," Ptolemy said as he rose from his bow and grinned. "That was a colt we got in from the northern piedmont a few days ago, and I was hoping to have him trained as a gift to you for use in the Theban campaign. He's bull-headed as a young ox, though, and I don't think I can have him trained before we leave for the summer operations. So far it seems he's impossible to ride, and he may have to become a routine chariot horse."

"He's too good a colt to let go to waste, Father. Let me try to ride him." A prince who had been sitting quietly on a little gelding behind the king's mount spoke these words. He had curly blond hair, and he was not yet old enough to grow a beard.

King Philhippos eyed his son skeptically. "What ever makes you think you could stay on that horse when your teachers Ptolemy and Hephaestion can't do it?"

"They taught me well, Father. But *hubris* caused by their rivalry with each other has gotten in the way of their horse sense." He winked at Hephaestion, who rolled his eyes and nudged Ptolemy with his elbow. "I saw something about Bull Head that they didn't. Can I have him if I can stay on his back?"

The king looked at his two *hipparchoi*, who stood with arms crossed and wearing devious smiles. "What do you think, fellas? Should we give him a crack at it?"

"Certainly, Sire," Ptolemy answered enthusiastically. "If the prince can stay on this horse for one minute, he can have him, and I'll even throw in the groom for good measure!"

"Bring Bull Head back to the pen," the king ordered, "and we'll see if the Prince of Macedon has been hoodwinked by his own *hubris*!"

So poor Stinky led me back into that horrible place for the fourth time. The blond boy was waiting there for me, and I wondered how many monsters he had brought with him. Stinky took a good hold on my halter and tried to prepare himself for my next bullheaded tantrum.

"Turn him around," the prince instructed as he brushed blond curls away from his eyes. "That's right; point him into the sun. There, there now, Bull Head," he said to me as he patted me on the neck and scratched me behind the ears. "Isn't that better now, Bull Head? I'm going to make all the monsters go away, and then we can go for a nice walk together. You don't see boogies now, do you, Bull Head?"

No, I didn't see any monsters. I could hardly see anything because the sun was in my eyes and I had to blink several times just to see where I was. The next thing I knew he was on my back and had eased my reins so that I could drop my head and take a look at the ground. All I could see there was brightly lit dirt. No monsters oozed out of the earth to snatch at me! By the gods, he had done it! He had made the monsters go away!

"Will you look at that!" Hephaestion exclaimed. "I do believe, Ptolemy, that you have just parted with one fine horse and one able-bodied slave!"

"Damned if you haven't," King Philhippos declared. He was smiling from ear to ear. "I don't know how in Hades he did that, but you men are obviously good teachers!"

I heard the elated prince shout from atop me. "I can have him ready for the Theban Campaign, Father. Will you give me a command?"

"Maybe so," the king shouted as the prince led me through the gate into an open field. "But you'll have to tell us how you did that!"

"He was afraid of his shadow," the boy called back. "Now he knows that there are no boogies trying to get him!"

My shadow, thought I as we raced across the meadow. *Well I'll be! What other surprises do you have for me, blond boy?"*

***

The answer to that last question came soon enough, because the prince took me into immediate training at his palace near Pella, the capital city of his father's kingdom. He rode me himself, and we trained in fields and forests and mountain paths. We galloped through villages, where people and pigs and chickens went screaming and fluttering out of our pathway. We jumped over logs and rocks and tramped through rivers and burning haystacks, and people would leap from behind wagons and trees to try to frighten me. The prince was in charge of a large contingent of palace guards, which included horse cavalry, charioteers, and foot soldiers called *peltasts*. He loved to put all these troopers to work creating mock battles so that he and I and his companions could train in realistic settings. My blond young master made me steady up and pay attention to his commands while foot soldiers pelted us with clods and onions and cabbages and whacked me on the rump and legs with their long spears while they all yelled and pounded their shields to mimic the sounds of battle. I became impervious to fear whenever the prince was astride my back.

And after a long day's work we would return to my splendid stall and paddock at the palace grounds, and the prince would bathe and brush me while he talked to me about the glory that we were soon going to experience. Stinky, who had himself been cleaned up, slept on a mat in a little room next to my stall, and was with me every minute to tend to my meals, my tack, my bedding and my grooming. I felt pretty important, and I didn't really understand why Stinky worried so much about everything. Yes, he always had to run alongside me to take my reins if the commander had to get off for any reason, but he wasn't a soldier, so what did he have to worry about? Beside that, King Philhippos had left for the Thessalian front weeks before and had left his son and his troops-in-training at home where we were safe.

One morning the prince came into the stable with a handful of exquisitely sharpened knife blades. He gave one to Stinky and told him to go out and cut all the hair off his face. Stinky obeyed, of course, and soon returned with milky white shaven cheeks and chin. I was surprised at how handsome he looked without that scraggly red beard.

"My theory is now proven correct," the blond prince opined as he studied Stinky's smooth profile. "All men are much more attractive if their faces are clean shaven! Henceforth all of my companion troops will have to sport that clean tough look."

Ptolemy and Hephaestion arrived from Thessaly that same afternoon with a message that the prince had long awaited. The king was ordering his son to bring his troops up in reserve for battle at Amphissa. If the Thebans and their Athenian allies could be routed at Amphissa, all of Southern Greece would be open for Philhippos to invade and force into his confederation of former city-states.

The prince had his command, and his first order to his two dear friends and chief *hipparchoi* was to shave their faces and trim their shoulder-length locks. "See how civilized my groom looks, Ptolemy! You and Hephaestion need to be handsomer than a slave. After all, we are shortly going to be famous, and the sculptors can carve our likenesses much more easily if they aren't encumbered by wads of hair." And so our cavalry unit departed for Thessaly with smooth-shaven riders astride and smooth-shaven frightened non-combatants alongside. I, of course, had no idea that this new look was the first of its kind in the history of warfare.

It took several days to get to the mountain pass where King Philhippos' army was preparing to break through into Southern Greece. The main Theban and Athenian armies were entrenched on a plain called Chaeronea, below Amphissa, and were willing to die to the last man to prevent Philhippos from advancing any farther south. When the blond prince caught sight of his father's rear guard, he rushed his eager cavalry forward to the king's headquarters and left poor Stinky and his supply train on the dusty mountain trails.

I am sure we cut a dashing figure as we rode up to the cliff edge where the king surveyed the battle. But the king was not smiling when my rider cheerfully announced his presence.

"I'm here, Father! Where do you want me to attack?"

"Where is your non-combatant support?" the king asked.

"What?" my rider answered. "You mean the grooms and the baggage train?"

"That is precisely what I mean. Where are they? Are they safe?"

"Well, certainly they're safe, Father. They are two miles behind the lines!"

"Oh, you mean they're back there where enemy infiltrators can kill all your grooms, steal all your food and wagons, burn all your tents and tack, and appropriate all your reserve weaponry?"

"How could such a thing happen if we're winning this war, Father!"

"We haven't won it yet, Son, and if you don't go secure your supply train we aren't going to win it."

"But I'm ready to fight the Thebans right now, Father!"

"No, you're not, Son. Now go gather your supplies and come to this war prepared, or I'll relieve you of your command."

Even I was embarrassed for my *hipparchos*, and I trotted briskly back down the mountain when he turned me toward the rear lines.

The king turned toward the battle that was raging below his perch, and finally smiled as he saw the Theban armies retreating toward their stronghold on the Chaeronea Plain. "There will be a war council tonight after sundown," he called after his departing son. "Get your supply lines in a secure place on the left flank, and be at that meeting for a discussion of tactics!"

***

My prince was almost in tears from embarrassment and frustration. A major battle had been won without him, all because he hadn't come prepared. He personally supervised the building of our camp, and Stinky was there with me with a sack of grain, a bucket of water, and all the hay I could eat. My blond *hipparchos* double-checked every detail, and ordered Ptolemy and Hephaestion to recheck everything again while he attended the war council with his father. I was happy to see that he was more upbeat when he returned from the meeting. I ate and drank and eavesdropped on the conversation between the prince and his two warrior friends while Stinky slept fitfully near my feet. Stinky knew, and I was about to learn, that tomorrow was going to be urgently eventful.

"Our horses are tougher than theirs, and we can form ranks in the rocky foothills on our left. We'll move toward the battle line without actually entering the plain, and the Thebans won't expect us to attempt cavalry maneuvers from such rough terrain. They'll be partly correct, of course. I hope they dig in well in front of us. Because, at the right moment, we are going to go around them and destroy them from the rear. You will take the light cavalry, Hephaestion, and go around them on the far left where the terrain is steep and rocky. Our light ground troops will offer a frontal attack to the left flank when I give the signal, and we'll squeeze the life out of them."

"But how are *you* going to get behind them," Hephaestion asked. "The best Athenian *hoplite* heavy infantry will be occupying the center of the field, and they can withstand any kind of cavalry charge you can offer."

Campfire light illuminated the biggest grin I had ever seen on my master's face. "You just wait and see," he said. "My father is a military genius, and I am learning quickly from him. Just don't let anybody get anxious and charge the enemy before I give the signal."

***

RD Weilburg

In the morning mist we moved down into the valley to do battle with the Thebans and Athenians. The Theban heavy infantry faced us on our left, and the Athenian heavy infantry occupied the center of the valley and their awesome squadrons, called phalanges, extended far to the right side. King Philhippos faced the Athenians with an army of maneuverable infantry called *hypaspistai* in the center of the valley, and heavier infantry on the far right flank. All of the Macedonian cavalry was on the left, and the rider astride my back was in charge of the entire contingent.

The din of battle was worse than anything I ever encountered in training maneuvers! There were horns and whistles blowing and men shouting from every direction. Whole armies would pound on their shields rhythmically, and the sound created could jolt the thunder gods from slumber! Nobody was tossing cabbages and onions this time! The simultaneous snapping of slings sounded like explosions, and the bronze bullets flung at the enemy made a high-pitched wheeze as they plummeted through the air. The missiles would clang off the *hoplite's* shields, after which the enemy troops would all shout defiant vulgarities in unison while their own archers sent barrages of arrows back at us. But there was no sound of charging cavalry, because my rider sat quietly on my back and watched the developments on the far right of the battlefield as his father's *hypaspistai* made a major charge at the Athenian center line.

The Macedonians ran up to within a few feet of the spear-tips of the heavily armored and entrenched Athenian phalanx. They threw their short heavy javelins into the enemy ranks, which rankled the target troops more than injuring them. When the angered enemy rose from their shield positions to give battle, the Macedonian *hypaspistai* turned and ran. And then an amazing thing happened.

As the Athenians on our right began to chase our retreating *hypaspistai*, the enemy infantry in the center of the battlefield thought that all of the Macedonian lines had broken and immediately lunged toward that side of the plain. They ran right by us, and left a huge gap in the position that they were supposed to be holding. Frustrated Athenian officers waved and shouted at their troops to hold their lines, but the excitement of having a foe on the run overcame discipline, and the entire center of the battlefield was suddenly left undefended. I felt heels urging my flanks and knew that it was time to charge! We left Stinky and the other grooms standing in dust as our cavalry plunged through the undefended center and quickly turned left behind the Theban lines. Hephaestion came charging out of the hills with his horsemen on the far left to meet us, and we had the entire enemy flank surrounded. The sixteen-foot-long spears of the enemy could not be pointed in two directions, and we ran through and over the trapped infantrymen. Javelins and rocks and bullets and arrows were flying everywhere, swords slashed against shields and bodies, and men grunted and shouted and screamed. When exhausted Thebans finally had their fill of carnage, they dropped their weapons and fell onto the ground in surrender. Hephaestion's unit then charged downfield to capture the Theban and Athenian supply trains and conscript the non-combatants that managed them.

Meanwhile, King Philhippos' feint had come to an abrupt halt. His disciplined troops turned to face the oncoming Athenians, who thought they were chasing frightened quitters. The heavily armored Athenians had chased them for over half a mile lugging spears, swords, battle-axes and heavy shields, and they suddenly ran out of energy. And just as the Macedonian *hypaspistai* turned to engage the tired enemy, our cavalry, keyed by defeat of the Thebans, now charged into the Athenian rear. It was a rout, as the Athenians suffered the same humiliation as the Thebans had, and my prince was the general in charge of the victorious cavalry! And what a *hipparchos* he was! He had led me through a hell that was far worse than the monster-infested terror of my youth, and I am alive to tell about it!

After the Battle of Chaeronea, all of Southern Greece lay open for Philhippos to occupy, and, for the first time in history, Greece would be a unified nation under his aegis. The king's dream was to invade Persia, but unfortunately he did not live to realize that ambition. His son would have to do it in his stead.

And I, known by my historic name, *Bucephalus*, got to help him do it. In the ensuing fifteen years, I carried my blond prince across three continents as he conquered most of the civilized world. From Greece to Egypt to Persia to India, I was the bull-headed steed who enabled my *hipparchos* to execute his strategies to perfection. Ptolemy and Hephaestion came along to help, too, and became famous in their own right. My master's name, as you may have guessed, was Alexander!

Oh, and Stinky came along, too; but if he had a real name, I never learned it.

ONE DAY OF NOT PLAYING FAIR WITH ZACHARY

Belle Blaise was a sweet untypical twelve-year-old girl who achieved excellent grades, did her chores, and respected the wishes of her parents. Her parents, in turn, allowed her to have an expensive hunter horse named Lothar, which Belle cherished more than life itself. Belle's horse trainer was Billie Tinkler, who was considered one of the finest horse trainers in the United States and who also was known around all circuits as a really good guy. Billie was a little light in the tennies, but his sexual preferences did not in any way interfere with his job performance or relationship with his youthful customers.

Kaitlyn Katz was the diametric opposite of Belle. Her parents had suppressed urges of infanticide by desperately searching for a diversion to preoccupy their child from mischief. Unfortunately for the discipline of Equestrian Sport, they bought her a horse. Worse yet, they stabled their miscreant with Zackary van Slang, who was the crookedest horse trainer to ever wield a quirt.

Zachary's knowledge of horsemanship was keen enough to keep him in the business, and he would have qualified as a top trainer even if he didn't work overtime trying to figure out ways to cheat. His desire to win superceded all moral and ethical instincts, and he was frequently tired because he had spent the entire night dreaming of ways to cheat even if it if concerned a sport in which he didn't participate. He thought about devising a football field with hydraulic tilts so the opposing team would always be running uphill. He dreamt of basketball hoops that would change diameter with a remote control. He had a bass in a tank behind his house that he force-fed like a Strasbourg goose; it was his intention to enter a fishing contest and carry the potential behemoth to the contest in a secret well beneath his boat. His prowess for mischief on the hunt field was both unique and legendary, and it caused this story to be written.

 The Brotherhood of Superannuated Uncles held a large and prestigious four-day hunter and jumper charity horse show every year. Winners of BSU championships could actually earn enough prize money to pay show expenses, and they received triple points for state and national championships as a bonus. The show was therefore heavily entered by participants who had state, district, and national championships in their sights. Enter Belle Blaise and Kaitlyn Katz, who, to this point in the state championship standings, were evenly tied and intent on sweeping the determining BSU points. Since both girls were juniors and school was still in session, the classes in which they were entered would run heavily on Saturday and Sunday, with many classes being back to back, and stakes classes running late in the evening. Zachary van Slang therefore had two days to figure out ways to cheat to Kaitlyn's advantage, which was one day more than he needed to do it masterfully, surreptitiously, and in timely fashion.

 Belle Blaise stayed with her mother at a motel about three miles from the show grounds. They had driven the four-hour drive from home the evening before, after Belle properly attended her Friday school session. Belle's mother, Bethany, always willingly chauffeured her daughter to the shows, but she was never one to be hurried at breakfast. She sat in the motel dinette drinking her coffee and eating some commissary chef's lame rendition of Egg's Benedict while Belle fidgeted in her seat.

"Mo-ther! I haven't gotten to school Lothar yet, and my class is going to start in an hour. Billie is going to be really perturbed if we don't get schooled properly."

"Billie tuned up Lothar for you last night, Belle. That horse will be smooth as glass when you go into the ring. Now just give me a minute to finish my coffee and we'll go. There isn't any point to sitting on that horse for half an hour and getting him all nervous before you go in the ring."

"But I have to walk the course with Billie, Mom! We have two rounds back to back, and I have to be sure I know both courses. I would be so *dissed* by everybody if I went off course! Mo-ther, my championship is on the line here!"

Bethany Blaise gulped her last dreg of coffee and went out to the car with her daughter. "Do you have everything, Belle? Helmet, gloves, rear end?"

"Mo-ther."

They headed to the show grounds with plenty of time to spare, and the little girl sat back in the car seat and finally relaxed. Bethany stopped the car at a traffic light near a freeway overpass, and Belle commented on the homeless men that were selling flowers and newspapers alongside the intersection.

"Look at those poor men, Mother. Why do they have to live like that?"

"They're down on their luck, Honey. See, some of them are carrying signs saying that they'll work for food."

"That one has a sign that says WILL DO ANYTHING. He sure is creepy looking."

Bethany diverted her eyes from the traffic signal to look at the man, who was wearing cutoff jeans and a neon green tee shirt. He had blue tattoos on both arms and both legs and was grinning bizarrely as he pointed his signs at passersby.

"Whoa, you're right, Honey. He looks like trouble looking for a place to happen."

The light changed, and Bethany drove on across the intersection. A police siren and flashing red lights suddenly materialized behind them.

"Oh no," Bethany said disgustedly. "Now what?" She pulled over to the side of the road and waited for the husky policeman to amble over to the car. She had already hunted through her purse and extracted her driver's license when he arrived. She handed it to him and asked a question at the same time. "What have I done, officer?"

"You haven't done anything, Madam," the officer said politely. "Which is the problem. You don't have an inspection sticker."

"What!" Bethany Blaise looked at her front window in disbelief. Sure enough, there was no inspection sticker in the lower left corner.

"I assure you there was one on there when I drove over last night," Bethany said with a genuinely perplexed tone. "Someone must have scrapped it off during the night, at the motel."

"Right, Lady," the cop sniggered. "Some skulker is going around scrapping off people's inspection stickers at motels in the middle of the night. Let me see your proof of insurance, please." He waited for her to produce the document and looked at it carefully.

"Look, Officer," Bethany said. "You can see where the stickum wasn't all scrapped off. There was a sticker on there last night. Do I look like a person who would drive around in a Lexus with no inspection sticker?"

"I guess you do, Lady, cuz there isn't one there."

Belle leaned over to the officer from her side of the car and began to cry enormous tears. "I am about to miss the most important horse show in my life because somebody sabotage my Mommy's car. Please, Mr. Policeman, can't you see that someone did this to us? Please, please let us go!"

The big cop could deal with annoyed women, but he couldn't handle a crying child. He handed the license and insurance papers back through the window and stepped back. "Okay, y'all, be on your way. But I'll write you a ticket as long as your arm if there isn't an inspection sticker on this car next time I see it."

Bethany and Belle parked at the grounds and ran across a vast no-parking area to get to Billie Tinkler's tack room. Lothar, Belle's fancy white-socked chestnut gelding, was saddled and patiently waiting for his rider while Billie Tinkler flitted around him in a pluperfect snit.

"Where in the hell have you been, you miscreants!" Billy Tinkler spoke in a high-pitched frustrated tone. "Your class has already started and you don't even know the course!"

"We got stopped by a cop, because someone scrapped off our inspection sticker," Bethany explained in a very perturbed voice. "We're lucky we made it at all, Billie."

Billie Tinker suddenly became very calm and focused. "Zach! That's gotta be a Zachary van Slang trick. I can smell it." He legged Belle up onto her horse and patted her on the thigh. "Okay, Honey. You be cool now. Let's go learn these two courses and blow the judge's socks off. It's going to be okay; you're still gonna win."

The stress of the delay and the hurried course memorization was enough to cause Belle to get a little too close to the first fence, and she knew she hadn't put down a winning ride. But she gutted up and rode the second round perfectly. She was called in second on the first round, and was still seething when she led Lothar out of the ring with a red ribbon behind Kaitlyn Katz.

"Get a grip," Billie said sternly. "They're about to call the order for the second round's ribbons, and I'm sure you won it. At least no tricks were pulled on us during the second round."

Belle Blaise and Lothar were called out first for the second round, as Billie had predicted, but a satisfying surprise occurred when Kaitlyn Katz was called out third. Zachary van Slang ran over to the judge and asked to see her card Zachary gesticulated wildly with his hands while he rambled at the judge, but whatever he said didn't change the judge's mind. The order stood as called with the blue going to Belle and the yellow going to Kaitlyn. In the standings for championship, Belle was now ahead of Kaitlyn eight points to seven.

"Keep your guard up, Honey," Billie said to Belle, "and above all, keep your cool. It's going to get nasty from here."

Belle had no more classes until after the lunch break, so Bethany left the show grounds to get the car inspection sticker replaced on her Lexus. Belle remained on the grounds and joined some of her junior colleagues in the grandstand to watch the remainder of the morning's events.

Included in this crowd was Fiona Donaldson, the five-year-old daughter of two accomplished and very popular horse trainers, Sean and Mickie Donaldson; her nickname was Fifi. When she was old enough to walk, Fifi had been turned loose by her parents to pretty much do what she wanted, as long as she stayed out of the way. Fifi was born with the genes and burning desire to be a horseback rider, and if she wasn't on her pony at home, she was at ringside at the horseshows dreaming of the day she could ride in a class. Everyone at every horse show, children and adults alike, knew and looked after Fifi. Fifi was a skinny little kid, and the show parents fed her sodas and hotdogs and hamburgers in a steady stream, but she never gained an ounce because she burned off energy as fast as she stoked it in. In a nutshell, she was a cute little ragamuffin that everybody loved.

Fifi sat next to Belle, who shared a box of popcorn with her, on the first row of the grandstand seats to watch a round of older junior hunters. "My daddy has a horse in this class," Fifi said matter-of-factly. "But he isn't going to win."

Belle looked at the little girl curiously. "Why do you say that, Fifi?"

"Zach's horse is going to win. You watch, Belle."

Zachary van Slang was standing with Kaitlyn Katz near the rail opposite the second fence, which was a white three-foot double oxer. They were both standing very quietly with large bamboo toothpicks in their mouths watching the first horse of the class approaching the oxer. The horse was coming in perfect stride, but it unexpectedly added a stride in front of the fence and crow-hopped over it; the rest of the trip was perfect, but one blown jump was enough to miss a ribbon. Oddly, the next horse swung his rump to the inside and was urged on over the fence by a Herculean effort of his skilled young rider, but the trip was automatically a looser. Zachary and Kaitlyn stood by the fence motionless, except for the occasional adjustment of their toothpicks.

"Here comes my daddy's horse," Fifi said.

The teenage rider guided her big bay gelding over the first fence with smooth precision and hit her stride perfectly to approach the second fence. Then she flinched and almost fell off. She recovered to make it over the oxer, but there was no perfection in the jump, and she missed her lead going into the turn to the third fence. Zachary and Kaitlyn both turned toward the grandstand seats with suppressed grins on their faces.

"See, I told you so," Fifi said. "Zach ruined her trip. I'm gonna go tell my daddy." The little girl jumped up and ran around the rail to the warm-up paddock where her father was trying to console his very disappointed young rider.

"A bee or something stung me on the neck," the teenager was saying to her trainer as she forced back tears. "I lost my concentration. I blew the fence, didn't I?"

"And your lead, too," Sean answered disgustedly. "You might as well put him up, Honey, because you're out of the ribbons." He felt a tug on his trousers and looked down. "You're not supposed to be out here, Fifi. Go back to the stands right now before somebody runs over you."

"But Zack cheated, Daddy. He shot at your horse with BB's."

Sean's eyes narrowed. "Wait a sec, Sandy," he said to his rider, who had dismounted and was preparing to lead her horse back to his stall. "Let me see that bee sting." He looked at her neck, and saw a tiny red bruise; there was no allergic swelling around it. Sean glanced over toward the grandstand and saw Zack and Kaitlyn standing just beyond the first fence, and he knew what they had done. "Come with me," he said to Fifi. "Your daddy has a job for you."

Sean Donaldson led Fifi to the concession stand, where he bought her a quart-sized cola that was half ice chips. "Okay, Fifi, you go over and do what I told you. Be sure you wait til the horse clears the first fence." He grinned as he reached down to kiss her on the cheek. "I promise I'll buy you another Coke," he called after her as she ran toward her place in the grandstand.

"Oh, can I have a taste of your Coke," Belle asked Fifi as she sat down.

"Yes, but just a little one, please, Belle. You can have a big drink of my next one," she said with a smile as she tucked the large drink between her knees and watched a horse come into the ring and begin a circle to the first fence. As the horse approached the fence, Fifi stood up on the seat and got a good grip on the drink. The horse cleared the fence and took one stride toward the oxer as Zack and Kaitlyn both adjusted their toothpicks. Fifi flung the icy drink, which hit Zachary van Slang square in the back. When the freezing cold liquid sloshed through his shirt and breeches, he gasped from the shock of it and swallowed a mouthful of number twelve lead shot that he had tucked under his tongue. The ice also hit Kaitlyn, but she spit the shot in her mouth out over the railing into the dirt. The horse passed by and took the second fence perfectly.

Zachary turned around to see who had nailed him, but curtailed his urge to strike out when he saw that it was little Fifi. "What the hell did you do that for, Fifi," he screamed through a spasm of coughing."

"You were flicking BB's at the horses with those bamboo toothpicks," she said with an innocent smile. "I know how to put a BB in my teeth and flick it. My daddy taught me when I was a little girl! I'm not going to tell the judge, Zach. But you'd better not do that any more."

Shortly, Fifi was sitting in the stands sharing her new drink with Belle and the other kids.

Bethany Blaise returned from the service station in time to take her daughter and some of the other children to lunch at the show facilities concession stand.

Billie Tinkler came to their table and gave Fifi a kiss on top off her disheveled head. "You are hero of the day, Fifi," he said, laughing. But we still have to look out. Old Zack is mad and will get nastier than ever before this show is over. We have to watch for something really illegal, and maybe we can get rid of him permanently."

"So far today I've paid thirty dollars for a new inspection sticker and Belle lost over two hundred dollars in prize money because of that guy's antics. I'm gonna deck the little weasel if I catch him at any shenanigans," Bethany said seriously.

"Well, don't let your guard down," Billie said. "Belle, you'd better go tack up your horse for the hack class; I'll meet you at the in-gate."

Belle got up from the table and headed to their tack room to get Lothar ready for the under saddle class. Fifi ran after her. They found Lothar cross-tied in the aisle, where a groom was giving his red rump a good brushing. Fifi helped Belle with her bridle and saddle, and when the public address system announced the class, Belle was ready to lead him to the in-gate of the ring. Lothar was an animated daisy-clipper, and was by far the best-moving horse in Belle's division. The class would take place out in the center of the large ring, which had been cleared of all jumps. Not only were Belle and Lothar not likely to make a mistake, Zachary van Slang wouldn't be close enough to any of the equine participants to attempt a misdeed. Five points for a blue ribbon for Lothar was almost guaranteed as Belle Blaise led him down the shed row.

Ten Horse Tales

Belle and Lothar had to pass down Zachary van Slang's shed row as they proceeded to the ring, and they found their progress stopped by a horse that was cross-tied across the aisle. Kaitlyn Katz was busily applying hoof oil to her gelding's feet.

"Oh, excuse me, Belle," Kaitlyn said with a sugary smile. She undid the cross tie so Belle and Fifi and Lothar could pass.

"They've called our class, Kaitlyn," Belle said with her usual kindness. "You'd better get him saddled and get to the ring."

As Lothar passed by, Kaitlyn quickly reached up and poured hoof oil over Belle's saddle. "Oh, thanks, Belle," she said sweetly. "I'll be right there. Good luck!"

Billie Tinkler's horses *always* arrived at the in-gate perfectly tacked up, so he didn't even glance at the saddle before he legged his young rider up into it. Belle was through the gate and officially in the class before she realized she was sitting on oozy slick goo. She felt the oil seep through her britches as the judge instructed the contestants to walk on. Belle gripped Lothar's sides with her legs to keep from sliding off, and the flashy chestnut thought he was supposed to trot. Belle's class was over before it began; she reined the confused Lothar back to a walk and, standing in her stirrups and suppressing tears, asked the judge to be excused from the ring. She headed for the exit without waiting for the judge to reply.

Belle dismounted while the paddock master opened the gate and led Lothar out of the ring into the midst of her mother, her trainer, and a half-dozen friends.

"What now?" her frustrated trainer said angrily.

"Look at my saddle!" Belle responded with quivering chin. "Somebody poured grease all over it. It's already in my underwear!"

"This is intolerable, Billie!" Bethany Blaise exclaimed. "This is supposed to be a gentle sport, and my little girl is being assaulted mercilessly. I demand that you protest to show authorities. We are getting to a point of perversion here!"

Ten minutes later the class was over, and Billie and Bethany were consulting with the show steward, the show manager, and the judge. All three of the latter were sixty-five-year-old ladies who had each been on the horse show scene for over half a century. They listened to Billie Tinkler because he was respectable and polite, but they made it very clear that the class had been run fairly and Kaitlyn Katz had won it.

"Look," the steward said, "we don't know who sabotaged your rider, so we can't penalize the whole class for it. You can't prove that any one individual did this, so which of the sixteen other riders should we penalize."

"Let's do the class over," Bethany suggested.

The show manager wiped perspiration from her brow. "We are going to be pushing it close to finish the day's classes by midnight, and there'll be a huge fine from the national association if we run overtime. We simply can't repeat a class. Look, we've already got most of the jumps set for the first jumper class of the day. We can't clear the ring for a repeated flat class. And I agree that you can't punish all of the current ribbon winners because one person was sabotaged."

"Well, I'm horrified that such things are happening at a prestigious horse show," the judge said. "I will refuse to judge any individual who I suspect is cheating or has cheated during this show."

"Well," Billie Tinkler said disgustedly, "you'd better keep a sharp eye on Zachary van Slang and that little Katz girl. "They haven't placed legitimately in a class today."

"I can sue you for a statement like that, you little twit!" Zachary van Slang had walked up and insinuated himself into the conversation. "Your knickers are in a twinkle-toed knot because your horses simply can't beat mine, Billie." He stared the judge squarely in the eye. "These people are impugning my integrity, Gladys, and you shouldn't be standing here listening to this prejudiced crap."

"Shut your mouth and go mind your business, Zack. I'll listen to any legitimate grievance that is presented to me, and I think a child's butt coated with hoof oil is reason enough to be suspicious of dirty play. If I find out that you had anything to do with this, or if I detect any other of your shenanigans for the rest of this show, I'll see to it that you don't set foot on any show grounds anywhere in this country for the next century!"

Rebuffed but not chastised, Zachary walked away with a smirk on his face.

Mollified, but down four points in the Junior Hunter Under-Fourteen-Years Championship standings, Billie, Bethany and Belle walked back to their stabling area wondering how they would ever make up the deficit. There would be one hunter class in the afternoon and the hunter stake during the evening performances. If Belle won them both, for ten points, and Kaitlyn was second in both, for six points, they would be tied for the championship with eighteen points apiece. Any slip by Belle that allowed Kaitlyn to get tied above her would automatically extinguish the championship quest.

Bethany Blaise decided to take Belle back to the motel to change into a clean pair of riding breeches while the afternoon jumper classes were taking place. As they got out of their car, they were surprised to see coming out of the motel restaurant the same burly police officer that had stopped them that morning.

"Well hi there," he said jovially. "How did the horse show go for y'all today?" As he spoke he glanced at the windshield of Bethany's Lexus to see if the inspection sticker had been replaced.

"It's there now," Bethany said with chuckle, "but the jerk who scraped off the old one has been giving us unshirted hell today. Look what he did to my child." She took Belle by the shoulders and spun her around so the officer could see her oil-soaked riding breeches."

"That is bordering assault," the officer said sanguinely. He pulled a business card out of his shirt pocket and handed it to Bethany. "Here, I'm Officer Grumworth. Give me a call if you catch him picking on any more little kids. He might not like meeting me so much."

Bethany tucked the card in the pocket of her blouse and took Belle to their room to change clothes.

The afternoon schedule of jumper classes was just ending when Bethany and Blaise got back to the show grounds, so they sat in the bleachers with their usual coterie and watched the jump crew remove all the brightly colored jumper obstacles and replace them with natural or white fences, coops, and walls. After the obstacles got placed and decorated with flowers and greenery, Belle would be meeting Billie Tinkler on the field to memorize the course and pace off all the distances and predetermine how many strides Lothar would need to take between each fence.

"Look, Mother," Belle said in a low voice. "That green shirted tattooed guy we saw this morning is working with the jump crew!"

Bethany looked over to see the shorts-clad colorfully tattooed man helping to install an obstacle on the course. "Looks like he got himself a job," she said to her daughter. "I guess he really did want to work."

The green-shirted laborer helped four other men set the heavy replica of a chicken coop near the rail and place it exactly as the course designer instructed. After the other men left, he went to the crew's truck and got some potted trees and placed them at each end of the pyramidal white structure to add an esthetic appeal. He knelt in the dirt and packed soil around each plant so it would sit firmly in its place. While he knelt there, he also attended to some other business that no one who was watching suspected. He attached a wire to part of the coop and ran it to the ringside rail, burying it in the dirt as he went. Later, when the contestants were all out walking the course with their trainers, the green-shirted man, now outside of the ring, found the end of his wire and ran it under the seats into the darkness below the grandstand.

Billie Tinkler stayed with Belle from the moment Lothar left his stall until he entered the warm-up ring for the third over-fences class. He made sure that no one came within ten feet of his horse and rider. He suppressed an urge to kick dirt at Kaitlyn Katz's highly polished boots when she walked by with her gelding in tow, but was satisfied in knowing that she was in his sights and therefore not a threat to his rider.

Kaitlyn got on her horse, was schooled over two fences by her smug trainer, and trotted into the ring as the first horse in the class. She put down a breathtakingly beautiful ride; the kind of ride that a judge circles on her card and thinks, *Okay, now let's see who's going to be second in this class.*

Billie watched every ride, and after sixteen trips he knew that Belle's daisy-clipping knee-jerking Lothar would surprise even the venerable Judge Gladys if no tricks were played on his rider. Kaitlyn's trip may have been perfect, but perfection would be a relative concept if Belle and Lothar did their thing to their expected capabilities during this final trip of the class.

Belle and Lothar had ridden a wondrous trip as they came down a line along the grandstand to a big white coop. Two strides out, Belle and Lothar saw chickens everywhere. They emerged from the coop cackling, squawking and flapping wings as they ran helter-skelter over the hunt field. Unseen in the darkness behind the grandstand, the tattooed man in the green shirt reeled in his wire, chortling all the while.

Belle knew that she was immersed in an act of sabotage, but Lothar knew only that he was in the midst of a zillion crazy birds, and he gave serious thought to stopping. But the gutsy little rider took charge, urged Lothar to keep going, and took him over the coop through a flock of scattering fowl in perfect form. At her command, he switched leads in the turn and did his last line of fences in classic form. And old Judge Gladys immediately called her into the ring for the blue.

Zachary van Slang charged around the perimeter of the ring to the judge's stand in utter disbelief. "Gladys, have you lost your mind! The horse you tied first damned near stopped in that line! That's a five-stride line, and he took at least one more than that! I got this one on videotape, Gladys; you gotta change the call-out order!"

Old Judge Gladys smiled defiantly. "Your video will show a bunch of chickens running under my first place horse, won't it, Zack? Now I'm supposed to judge this show like it's a real hunt, right? That little girl and that big chestnut faced a true hunting obstacle and handled it with aplomb! The horse I tied second had a picture perfect ride, but she wasn't really riding to the hunt, was she? Was that your rider, Zack? She would have won if the last rider hadn't had such a wonderful challenge. Tough horse apples, Amigo! Now get out of here and let me judge the rest of my show."

Belle picked up five points for that round, and Kaitlyn picked up three. The score for the championship was now Kaitlyn fifteen, and Belle thirteen. Belle had to win the evening stakes class or she was out of the running. Billie Tinkler's plucky little rider could pull it off, but Billie and Belle both knew that tonight Zack would be pulling out all the stops for skullduggery.

Belle Blaise sat with her mother in the stands eating snacks and watching one round after another as she waited for her final class to be called. Fifi joined them, and watched trips for nearly half an hour without saying a word. Finally the little girl handed her bag of potato chips back to Belle and pointed across the ring.

"Uh oh, I see that bad man again."

"Where, Fifi," Belle asked. "What bad man?"

"See that guy with the green shirt? He's got pictures drawn all over his legs. I saw Zack give him some money and a little dog. He's going to do something bad."

Bethany again recognized the vagrant who had, for a while, worked with the jump crew. He was now sitting in the very end of the bleachers, near the warm-up ring, and he was holding a little mutt that was typical of the non-pedigreed throw-aways that populate city dog pounds. She decided to keep her binoculars on him for a few minutes to see what he was going to do, but he didn't do anything but sit there.

Bethany decided to stay in the stands when Belle got up to get ready for her class. She kept an eye on the green-shirted man.

Belle had been last out in the previous class, so she was first to ride in the stakes class. Once more she and Billie took every precaution to assure that her trip would go off without interference. She entered the ring, made her circle and rode for the first fence feeling that she was going to put down the best ride of her life. She committed to the first fence and a dog appeared from nowhere and began to bark and nip at her horse. She crow-hopped the fence, pulled Lothar up and dismounted while the ground crew chased the dog around the fences.

Belle Blaise was no longer a teary child; she was furious. "I protest," she yelled toward the judge's stand. "This is criminal, what they're doing to me!"

Judge Gladys and the steward both walked quickly to the in-gate and arrived just as Bethany did.

"I saw that guy throw that dog over the rail just as Belle started her round," Bethany asserted to the judge and steward. "This is truly a criminal effort to destroy my child's championship chances. I demand that she be allowed to start over. There aren't any other complete rounds yet, so there shouldn't be any excuses for not just starting this class over right now!"

"But it's like a hunter class, remember!" Again Zachary van Slang had appeared to argue his case. "Chickens and dogs discombobulate horses during the hunt. It's part of the game, Gladys; you said so yourself. This kid didn't complete the course, so she's disqualified."

"I'm the judge here, and I'll decide who's disqualified, Zack. We are going to restart this class and Belle Blaise will be the first horse out. That's my decision."

Zack turned to the steward. "I protest. Officially, I protest! The judge said that chickens contributed to the authenticity of the class, so should dogs."

"No, they shouldn't," the steward said officiously. "Dog's without leashes are specifically forbidden to be on these show grounds, or this hunt, if you will. There is nothing in the rules that forbid chickens, and I'm sure that you would have pointed that out to me when the chickens were running all over the place, had we made an issue of it. But dogs can't be here, and this kid is going to get to re-ride because of it." She turned to Belle. "Get on that horse and ride for your life, little girl. You may never get this lucky again."

"That's right," the judge said. "I don't care if a tornado takes the roof off this building, young lady; you get only one more chance."

Belle waited for the judge and steward to walk back to the judge's stand. When she heard the starting whistle blow, she indeed began to put down the ride of her life. But as she changed leads on the last turn for home, she really began to believe that the roof of the building was coming down. Somewhere alongside the huge arena someone was leaning on the blare-horn of an eighteen-wheeler van. The unrelenting blast caused the metal bleachers to hum in disharmony, and people within the building could feel their innards vibrating. Lothar thought he was going to Valhalla in a Wagnerian epiphany; he slowed to a trot and lifted his tail, but Belle set her boot heels into his flanks and he regained his composure to go over the last two fences perfectly. The horn stopped, and Belle, knowing that she had broken stride, came crestfallen out of the ring. She dismounted and began to unsaddle her horse.

"Don't do that," Billie Tinkler ordered. "Wait till everybody else goes. I think you're going to get called in."

"He broke stride, Billie," Belle reminded her trainer.

"I don't think the judge saw it," Billie said. "She was craning her neck to see where the noise was coming from."

Belle broke into a relieved grin. "Really, Billie. I didn't think old Gladys ever missed anything."

"She never misses anything she doesn't want to miss, Belle. Towel off your horse and look smart. You're going to win this class."

Billie Tinkler was right. Belle and Lothar got called in first, over Kaitlyn Katz. Which meant that Belle and Kaitlyn were tied for the championship with eighteen points apiece. There would have to be a hack-off, an under-saddle match performance between the two, with the judge's decision final for the championship.

Zachary van Slang stomped over to the judge's stand with the comportment of a rabid skunk. "You can't do this, Gladys! That chestnut horse broke stride in the last turn!"

"I didn't see her break any stride," the judge said as she looked over to the steward. "Did you see her break stride, Ethel?"

"I just heard a horn blowing," the elderly steward answered. "I didn't see the end of her trip. It must have been fantastic though, to finish in spite of that noise! I hope no horns blow during the hack-off."

Zachary was about ready to explode when he felt someone tugging on his shirt. He looked down into the serious face of five-year-old Fifi Donaldson.

"Hey, Zack," Fifi announced in her innocent little-girl voice. "That guy in the green shirt with the pictures all over him wants you to bring him his money or he won't blow the horn anymore. He's waiting in your truck."

Zachary left the premises so quickly that he appeared to dematerialize. Because the show was running so late in the day, the judge declared that the hack-off between Belle and Kaitlyn would take place the following morning, and the event would be conducted under the rules and regulations of any other class recognized by the national association; which meant that the horses were subject to testing after the event was completed. To Billie Tinkler, this meant there was plenty of time for Zachary van Slang to devise dastardly tricks to help Kaitlyn win the Championship; Billie's job was to eliminate Zack's opportunities entirely. He asked Bethany Blaise, his trainer friend Sean Donaldson, and the show grounds security chief to meet in his tack room to discuss strategy.

***

Zachary van Slang hid in the darkness behind the canvass curtain of his tack stall and waited patiently for the security guard to amble by on his rounds up and down the poorly lighted shed rows. The guard leisurely flashed his light into every stall to assure that its horse was okay; he finally disappeared into an aisle at the far end of the barn complex.

Zachary, carrying a coffee can, quietly stepped out of his tack room and slinked along the poorly lit shed row to Billie Tinkler's stalls. He noticed that Tinkler's tack room was closed up tightly as he passed it on his way to Lothar's stall, which was directly next to the tack room and shielded from the barn's nightlights by the tack room's canvass covering. He slid the stall door open and could barely make out Lothar standing in a back corner and snoozing by his water bucket. He petted Lothar on the neck gently, so as not to startle him, and Lothar gave him a soft snort.

"I've got a treat for you, Lothar," Zachary whispered as he poured a canful of strong coffee into the water bucket. "A little caffeine ought to sharpen you up good, huh boy? Shhh, I've got a little shot for you, too. You like procaine?" He extracted a syringe from his pants pocket and held it up near his face in the poor light to remove the plastic needle guard.

"I'm gonna tell on you." The child's high-pitched voice came out of the pitch-blackness of the opposite corner of the stall.

"I'm gonna tell on you, too." Another, slightly lower pitched voice came from the same corner.

Fifi and Belle had been silently sitting there in the dark anticipating Zachary's arrival and dirty tricks.

Zachary reacted by slipping the syringe back into his pocket and running to the stall door. He was met by the glare of a flashlight.

The girls' voices had triggered the alarm. Billie Tinkler, Sean Donaldson, Bethany Blaise and a security guard had been waiting in the tack room for their signal to rush out, and they slammed the stall door against Zachary as he tried to come through it. The guard then grabbed him by the arm and pulled him on out into the shed row. On her cell phone, Bethany dialed a number that she was reading from a card with a penlight.

Billie dashed into the stall to dump the water bucket before Lothar could take a drink from it. "You forgot your coffee can, Zach," he said as he kicked the can out of the stall door.

"I was just in there petting your horse," Zachary yelled nervously. "That ain't illegal. I'm going to sue the lot of you for assault!"

"You were trying to get my horse to test positive for caffeine," Billie Tinkler said.

Zachary crossed his arms defiantly. "You can't prove that, you little fairy flit. You just emptied the water bucket!"

"You'd better just shut your mouth before you get in more trouble," the security guard said.

"You're not even a real cop, buddy. I'm gonna nail you, too."

"*I'm* a real cop, *buddy*, and you're under arrest." This pronouncement came from Officer Grumworth, who had instantly responded to Bethany's call. He handcuffed Zachary and led him by the shoulder toward the barn exit.

"The syringe is in his pocket," Belle said. "He was going to poison my horse with procaine."

"Possession of a cocaine derivative is a serious offense, young man. Looks to me like you're in big trouble!"

"You can't search my pockets without a warrant," Zachary spat, panicking. "You can't prove anything on me."

In the bright lights of the squad car the outline of the syringe in Zachary's pocket was easy for everyone to discern.

"If you will all testify to the fact that that syringe is in his pocket as I'm taking him away, we'll have a warrant waiting for him when I get him to the station," Officer Grumworth said with a smile. "Meanwhile, I think your horses and your inspection stickers are safe. Now, Mr. van Slang, you have the right to remain silent, anything…"

***

On Sunday morning daisy-clipping Lothar went through his paces flawlessly underneath his confidently smiling rider. He was awarded the Championship Tricolor by Judge Gladys to the applause of Bethany, Fifi, Billie and a host of other well-wishers, including Officer Grumworth. Belle led her champion off to the testing barn, where, of course, he passed his last important test of the weekend.

THE LEETLE HORSE

Clifton Weicker flashed his owner's badge for the security guard and drove into the backside of Retama Race Park in Texas. He found a parking spot near barn 8, in the sun, of course, and walked across the road toward the building in the Sunday morning heat. He saw a horse that he knew well on the hotwalker between barns 8 and 9, and he saw his trainer standing alone, watching the chestnut colored horse move in his obligate mindless circle.

"Good morning, Parson," he said as he shook the trainers hand. "Did Capsacious come out of the race all right? Does he seem to be hurt?"

Parson Peabeck shook his head disgustingly. "Ain't nothin' wrong with him at all. He just decided to take a vacation last night. He'd never seen the butt end of another horse on the track, and I guess he just got curious. So he got to see nine butts last night. I hope he's satisfied."

"Well, he doesn't need to be vacationing in hundred-thousand-dollar stakes races. After winning his first three, why does he pick the big one to goof off?"

"Beats me, Mr. Weicker, but I'll get after him good if he tries to dog it again."

"Yeah, well, let's have the vet go over him with a fine toothed comb. If there's something wrong, I want to know about it now. I'm so disgusted I could cuss!"

"Enjoying your morning stroll, you lazy laddy?" This was the r-trilling voice of Petey O'Flanagan, who had ridden Capsacious the night before and had just strolled over from behind barn 9 to pat the big two-year-old colt on the rear as he passed around. "Good morning, Mr. Weicker, Parson. What are we going to do about our miscreant fellow? He cost us sixty thousand dollars last night. I stopped thinking about my ten per cent when he stopped to smell the flowers at the first turn."

"His little brain needs some motivational input," Weicker answered. "Maybe we ought to geld him."

"Not yet, Mr. Weicker," the wiry trainer replied quickly. "Petey and I will work this problem out. Maybe this big ol' fella just had an off night. He's nominated for that mile stakes for two-year-olds in Louisiana in two weeks. We'll van over there a few days early and give him another shot at a big purse. Meanwhile, I'll get the doc to go over him good."

***

The tingle of slot machines that wafted across the paddock to the saddling barn was interrupted by the drawl of the handicapper announcing his picks for the coming race. Clifton Weicker leaned on the fence and watched Parson Peabeck saddle Capsacious, who stood quietly in the open stall. Helping Peabeck to put on tack was a little old groom whom Weicker had never seen before. Weicker wondered who the new groom was, and why the groom that Peabeck had brought with him from Texas wasn't there, but he did not go into the saddling barn because he wanted to stay out of the busy trainer's way. After Capsacious was saddled, he was lead, bearing the number 4, into the paddock where Petey O'Flanagan was waiting to mount for the pre-race post parade. As horse and trainer entered the paddock, the handicapper announced the Texas colt's odds at forty to one. He had, after all, run dead last in his previous race.

Weicker walked over and listened to Peabeck's final instructions to his jockey: "Keep him up just off the pace, and whack him good if he tries to drop back. He's seen enough butts already."

Peabeck gave the jockey a leg up into his saddle, and O'Flanagan led his horse to the track entrance. There a pony rider led him into the post parade as the bugler announced the race with a brassy fanfare. Capsacious wowed the fans with spectacular conformation and elegantly quiet behavior as he was led past the grandstand, and he was steered into the starting gate without incident.

When the gates flung open, Capsacious bounded out into a slow canter, and as eleven other horses galloped away, a surprised and dismayed Petey O'Flanagan flailed his stick against the colt's enormous gluteus. Capsacious responded by throwing Petey over his head with one powerful thrust of his rump and then standing quietly beside the mortified little Irishman while he extracted himself from the track and brushed manure-laced dirt off his silks. Petey had never let go of the reins, so he pulled himself back onto the horse and was led off the track by an outrider. The outrider was kind enough to lead him out the back way, so he wouldn't have to face the fans and could avoid his frustrated owner and trainer for a few minutes.

The new groom, whose run to the gate was further than the distance that Capsacious had run on the track, met him at trackside. The panting old man didn't say a word; he took the reins and led the easy-breathing colt back to the barn.

***

RD Weilburg

The new groom's name was Rudolfo, and he had arrived at the barn about an hour before the race to replace Capsacious' regular groom, Ramon, who had gone to the hospital emergency room for treatment of an affliction caused by eating five dozen raw oysters. Rudolfo looked like he was eighty years old, but his groom's license said he was ninety. He was weather beaten and unshaven, but his clothes were freshly laundered, and he walked upright and moved with deliberation. He told Parson Peabeck that he had been around horses for many decades, and his deft handling of duties around the stable convinced the trainer that he was a last minute Godsend. Now the old man gave his new trust an un-earned bath and placed him in his cleanly prepared stall while the owner, trainer and jockey stood perplexed in the sandy aisle-way.

"No horse has ever humiliated me that way," Petey O'Flanagan said sheepishly. "I was on my arse in the dirt 'fore I could blink. I'm really sorry."

"Wasn't your fault, Petey," Peabeck assured. "He's just developed a stubborn streak that he's never demonstrated before. We'll just have to work it out of him when we get back to San Antonio."

"Maybe he does need to be gelded," Clifton Weicker said tersely.

"Oh, don't do that to him, Mr. Weicker," the groom said as he stepped out of the stall. "He's just got some *antagonishes* in his brains that have to get out. He'll come around, you just wait and see." The old man absently put his hands over his crotch, as if sympathizing with his threatened equine charge.

"Well, for sure I have some antagonisms in my own brain," Weicker answered with a hint of a smile, "and that silly horse is putting them there. His *noonies* are going into the bucket if he doesn't straighten up after he gets home."

"Can I go to San Antonio with him?" Rudolfo asked. "I know how to get the *antagonishes* out of his mind. I really do. Let me be his groom for now. I don't think Ramon is going to be well for awhile."

"Do you have a Texas license?" Peabeck asked.

"Sure," Rudolfo answered.

"Okay, Rudolfo. The van will pick him up tonight. You can ride home with him."

"Well, that's that, then," Weicker said. "I'll see y'all at Retama tomorrow afternoon. Get him home sound."

***

Clifton Weicker arrived at Retama Park shortly after noon the next day and found old Rudolfo, with a Texas Groom's License clipped to his shirt collar, taking Capsacious to his stall after a morning walk. Rudolfo waved at him and put the horse up securely before coming out to chat.

"Looks like he weathered his trip home okay, Rudolfo."

"Si, Mister Weicker. He slept late this morning after riding for nine hours. He's eating his lunch now. He's a very fine horse, Mr. Weicker. Are you going to campaign him for the Kentucky Derby?"

Weicker laughed loudly. "The Kentucky Derby! At the rate he's going, I won't be able to enter him in a Texas claiming race. It'll be weeks before he even gets into a race here if Parson and Petey can't get him straightened out."

Parson Peabeck walked out of his office and greeted his most expensive horse's owner. "Hi, Mr. Weicker. Looks like Capsacious got home sound as a dollar. Petey is going to come around tomorrow morning and start his retraining with an easy gallop."

"He ain't going to learn nothin' till the *antagonishes* get out," Rudolfo uttered quietly.

Peabeck gave his groom an irritated glance. "You got any ideas how to train this horse, Rudolfo?"

"No, Sir, Mr. Peabeck. I ain't no trainer. But I do know how to get rid of the *antagonishes*."

Peabeck looked at Weicker and rolled his eyes. "Okay, Rudolfo, tell me how you want to get rid of the *antago-whatevers*."

"He needs a visit with the *leetle* horse. The *leetle* horse will take away his *antagonishes*."

"You mean he needs a pony or a companion goat or something like that?" Weicker asked.

"No, Sir, Mr. Weicker. He needs a visit with the *leetle* horse. My *leetle* horse."

Peabeck sniggered. "Okay, Rudolfo, explain what you mean now. We've got lots of work to do around here and it ain't gettin' done while we're standin' around yakkin'."

"Let me get my *leetle* horse and show you. Is that okay with you, Mr. Weicker?"

"Whatever, Rudolfo. You've piqued my curiosity."

"Okay, I'll get him. Wait just a minute."

The old man walked briskly into the tack room and came out with a large grocery sack. It was a heavy-duty paper sack with reinforced paper handles and a big red Safeway logo. The sack was old and worn, and obviously contained most of Rudolfo's possessions. He rummaged around in the sack and lifted out a case about the size of a cigar box. The case was coated with shining white enamel, and there was an inlayed letter R on the lid. Rudolfo squatted in the sand beside Capsacious' stall door and carefully lifted the lid as he placed the container on the ground. He smiled up at Weicker and Peabeck as he reached into the case to extract a little statue of a horse.

The statue was carved in ivory, and the little horse's mane, hooves, and tail were lacquered bright cerise. The carved features of the horse's face and muscular conformation were exquisite.

"Hello, *leetle* horse," the old man said reverently. "I want you to meet my friend Capsacious today."

Rudolfo opened the stall and walked to the back wall while Capsacious was pulling a wad of alfalfa from his hay-net. The old groom patted an area of shavings with his shoe, and then carefully placed the little statue on the prepared place. He then walked out of the stall, closed the door, and stood beside Peabeck and Weicker to watch.

The latter two men gaped in amazement when Capsacious caught sight of the statue.

The big colt snorted and his eyes widened as he dropped the alfalfa from his mouth. He walked over to the figurine and sat straight back on his haunches. He then slowly lowered himself to the stall floor as he stretched his forelegs out in front of him to extend alongside the little horse. He pricked his ears forward and stared at the statue without moving a muscle.

A blue light began to emanate from the statue's eyes, and the cherry-colored mane suddenly extended straight up as the little tail arched over the figure's back in scorpion fashion. The ivory began to glow until it became ember-orange, and blue light from the eyes flickered brightly about the stall.

Capsacious stared at the glowing effigy for a full minute, and then reached out and touched it with his muzzle. Instantly the mane and tail dropped and the glow ceased. The blue from the eyes gradually faded, and the figure became a cold little ivory statue once more. Capsacious pulled himself to his feet, shook himself, and walked over to his hay-net to grab a mouthful of alfalfa as Weicker and Peabeck stood astounded and mute.

Rudolfo did not say a word. He stepped into the stall and carefully retrieved his little statue. He walked over to Capsacious and placed his arm around his neck and whispered something into his ear. The horse made a sound, almost like a purr, from deep in his throat, and continued chewing on his meal. Rudolfo exited the stall and placed the little horse back into its enameled case, and searched for a place in his Safeway sack to return the case. Only then did he look up to Clifton Weicker and his trainer and smile.

"There's a one mile allowance race here at Retama in six days," the old man said matter-of-factly. "Capsacious wants to run in it. He'll win by eight lengths."

***

Rudolfo proved to be prophetic. Petey O'Flanagan didn't have to touch his big colt with the whip. Capsacious willingly took the lead out of the gate and easily won by eight lengths. He also broke the Retama Park track record for the mile.

"He wants to go to California in October," Rudolfo said to Weicker in the winner's circle. "He wants to make you some money in a graded stakes race."

"I'll have to renew my California license," Weicker said, laughing.

"So will I," said Peabeck.

"So will I," said O'Flanagan.

"I already got one," said Rudolfo. "I love Santa Anita. And I can find a place to get a new sack"

***

Ten Horse Tales

Capsacious had no problem flying to California on a chartered air van. He arrived at Santa Anita ready to race in the two hundred thousand dollar Norfolk Stakes. If he could win it, he would have enough prize money to possibly be nominated for the Breeders Cup Juvenile in November. Derby thoughts also began to creep into the minds of Parson Peabeck and Clifton Weicker.

Nobody at Santa Anita had ever heard of the Texas-bred colt Capsacious, and the handicappers didn't take him seriously at all. There were a couple of fast California-bred colts entered in the race that were so intimidating that the race did not fill because owners didn't think they had a chance. Capsacious went to the starting gate with ten other competitors at odds of thirty-five to one, and caused a lot of joy-whoops for racing fans with the temerity to bet a long shot.

"We were so far ahead that I couldn't hear any hoof-beats behind me," Petey O'Flanagan shouted to Weicker and Peabeck over the din of the cheering crowd. He steered Capsacious, who was prancing excitedly, into the Winner's Circle to be photographed.

"Rudolfo! Come on in here and get in the win picture," Peabeck called to the old groom, who was walking rapidly toward the crowd just outside the fence.

"I don't like to be in pictures," Rudolfo shouted back over his shoulder. "I'll go clean his stall."

Because he won the race, Capsacious had to go to the test barn to be screened for drugs. Nobody had ever given him any, so he would pass that test with flying colors. Parson Peabeck then led him back to the barn by himself, because Clifton Weicker, now very respected in California as a horse owner, went to the Turf Club to celebrate his win with his family and track dignitaries. Peabeck was too busy getting his horse bedded down to worry about celebrating, so he left that activity to his owner.

Even Capsacious had to simmer down from his excitement. He understood full well that he had won the biggest race of his life, and he exhibited coltish exuberance when he saw Rudolfo filling his feed bucket.

Rudolfo kissed him on the muzzle as he entered the stall. "What a good boy you are, Niño! I have some good alfalfa for you. And look at these big juicy carrots I got for you at the Safeway!"

"He really loves you, Rudolfo," Peabeck said happily. "I hope you'll stay with him forever. He was a nanosecond off the track record today, and he's still only two."

"You gonna run him in the Breeders Cup in November, Mr. Peabeck?"

"Nah. He's too young. We're going to save his legs so he can run sound next year. He's going to catch a plane for San Antonio in the morning, and we'll give him a few weeks off in the Texas Hill Country. He can be just a horse for awhile."

"Thank you, Mr. Peabeck. He sure will appreciate that."

"I'm going to ride in the plane tomorrow, too. I'll see you in the morning, Rudolfo. Thank you for what you've done, whatever it was."

"You're welcome, Mr. Peabeck," the old man said, grinning. "Good night."

***

A couple of days later Clifton Weicker drove up to barn 8 to check on his colt. He saw him ambling around the hot-walker, so he walked over to watch him move. He was surprised to see Ramon standing studiously by the walker.

"Good morning, Ramon. Glad to see you back. Did you get all those oysters out of your system?"

"Did I ever, Mr. Weicker! I'll never eat another one as long as I live."

"Looks like Capsacious made his flight without incident. His feet okay today?"

"Feets is fine, Mr. Weicker. He's a tough guy!"

"Good, Good. Hey, where's old Rudolfo?"

"Dunno. You'll have to ask Parson about that. I ain't seen him since Capsacious got back.

Weicker frowned and headed for Peabeck's office. Peabeck stepped out as Weicker arrived at the door.

"Bad news, Mr. Weicker. Old Rudolfo stayed on the plane and copped a ride to Kentucky at your expense. Had his usual big grin and a new Safeway bag."

"Why did he want to go to Kentucky? It's fixin' to get cold there."

"He said he likes to check out the babies when they come in the winter. He's a crazy old coot. He fished around in that sack and found this for me to give to you." Peabeck handed a large manila envelope to his boss.

"What is this, Parson?"

"Beats me. Feels like pictures. I didn't open it, since it was for you."

Weicker tore the end open and looked inside. "You're right," he said. "There are some old photographs in here. Looks like Winner's Circle pictures."

Peabeck sidled over to observe the pictures as Weicker examined each one.

"Look at the rose garlands," Weicker exclaimed. "These are Derby winners."

"Yeah, we got Seattle Slew from 1977, Secretariat from 1973, Gallant Fox from 1930, and Sir Barton from 1919. They were all Triple Crown winners, as I remember. Who is this horse, Ben Brush, from 1896?"

He won the Kentucky Derby that year," Weicker answered. "There wasn't any Triple Crown then."

They studied the photos for some time. The Sir Barton and Ben Brush pictures were around one hundred years old, and they were brown and fading. But the joyous faces and the enormity of the rose garland told it all. Winning the Kentucky Derby was a once-in-a lifetime spectacular event, and there wasn't an owner or a trainer alive that wouldn't want to bask in the glory of that Winner's Circle in Louisville.

"So why did he pick these pictures to give you, Mr. Weicker. There have been a hundred and thirty-three Derby winners. Do you think he could have had something to...wait a minute. Wait...a...minute! Look, there he is! Standing right behind Seattle Slew in that crowd of onlookers behind the fence! Yeah, that's old Rudolfo. Hey look, he's back in the crowd in this Secretariat picture, too!"

"And this one," said Weicker, his face stricken with disbelief. "And this one, Parson. Look at him back there." Weicker's hands began to shake as he studied the Ben Brush picture. "And this picture was taken a hundred and twelve years ago, and there, by God, he is! No doubt about it. He doesn't look any different in any of them than he does now!"

"Holy mackerel, Mr. Weicker! What does this mean? He can't really be nearly two centuries old!"

Weicker grinned broadly and slapped the shaken Peabeck on the back. "It means, Parson, that we are going to the Kentucky

Ten Horse Tales

Derby, and there isn't any doubt in my mind that we're going to win it!

***

From his vantage point in the owner's boxes Clifton Weicker could observe a grand portion of the crowd that had assembled at Churchill Downs on the first Saturday in May. Every few minutes he searched through the fans with his binoculars, but he did not find anyone that resembled old Rudolfo. He even took his eyes from the eighteen thundering horses to scan the rails during the Derby, but saw no familiar old face.

Capsacious broke from the eighteenth pole position, which didn't hinder him for an instant. In four strides he was ahead of the pack, and Petey O'Flanagan moved him over to the rail before they got to the first turn. No other horse ever came close to him after that, and he became only the third horse in history to finish the Kentucky Derby in less than two minutes. He wasn't even breathing hard when he arrived at the Winner's Circle to be crowned with a garland of roses.

Weicker, Peabeck, and O'Flanagan celebrated and mixed with the crowd for hours after Capsacious returned to his stall. Not one of them chanced to lay eyes on old Rudolfo.

The following morning Clifton Weicker had breakfast in his hotel room to avoid the congratulating public. His waiter brought him the Louisville newspaper, and Capsacious was featured on the front page in a full-paged photo of the Winner's Circle. The big chestnut colt cut a magnificent figure standing under a smiling Petey O'Flanagan and beside joyous Weicker and Peabeck. Weicker's chest puffed with pride as he studied the picture of his magnificent horse and the adulating crowd of racing fans. Then a tear came to his eye. Near the front of the cheering mob was a little old man waving a red rose over his head and flashing an open-mouthed grin. In his left hand, which he was holding over his heart, was a little white horse figurine with a cherry-red mane and tail.

Made in the USA
Charleston, SC
13 November 2010